Dev pla ... **'s belly.**

"I can feel the baby kick you. I heard his heartbeat. But he still doesn't feel...real."

No, none of any of this felt real, most especially Dev touching her like this. But it would. At least the baby would. "He will. When you hold him. It'll feel more real than we can imagine."

Dev looked at Sarah. His gaze was searching. Open. There was something in those hazel eyes that had her breath catching in her throat.

But then he dropped his hands and stepped back. "We should get going. Don't want to be separated any more than we have to be."

Sarah could only nod, because her throat was too tight, and everything she'd dreamed of was too close. But instead of reaching for it, demanding it, she kept her mouth shut and followed Dev back out to the waiting room.

Because there was still a stalker torturing them, and no dreams were going to be realized in the midst of that...

CLOSE RANGE CHRISTMAS

NICOLE HELM

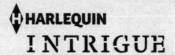

HARLEQUIN
INTRIGUE

I have to dedicate my fiftieth published work to computers,
because after watching the recent *Little Women* movie,
I know I couldn't have done it by pen.

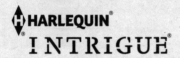

ISBN-13: 978-1-335-13683-1

Recycling programs
for this product may
not exist in your area.

Close Range Christmas

Copyright © 2020 by Nicole Helm

This edition published by arrangement with Harlequin Books S.A.

For questions and comments about the quality of this book,
please contact us at CustomerService@Harlequin.com.

Harlequin Enterprises ULC
22 Adelaide St. West, 40th Floor
Toronto, Ontario M5H 4E3, Canada
www.Harlequin.com

Printed in U.S.A.

Nicole Helm grew up with her nose in a book and the dream of one day becoming a writer. Luckily, after a few failed career choices, she gets to follow that dream—writing down-to-earth contemporary romance and romantic suspense. From farmers to cowboys, Midwest to *the* West, Nicole writes stories about people finding themselves and finding love in the process. She lives in Missouri with her husband and two sons and dreams of someday owning a barn.

Books by Nicole Helm

Harlequin Intrigue

A Badlands Cops Novel

South Dakota Showdown
Covert Complication
Backcountry Escape
Isolated Threat
Badlands Beware
Close Range Christmas

Carsons & Delaneys: Battle Tested

Wyoming Cowboy Marine
Wyoming Cowboy Sniper
Wyoming Cowboy Ranger
Wyoming Cowboy Bodyguard

Carsons & Delaneys

Wyoming Cowboy Justice
Wyoming Cowboy Protection
Wyoming Christmas Ransom

Stone Cold Texas Ranger
Stone Cold Undercover Agent
Stone Cold Christmas Ranger

Harlequin Superromance

A Farmers' Market Story

All I Have
All I Am
All I Want

Falling for the New Guy
Too Friendly to Date
Too Close to Resist

Visit the Author Profile page at Harlequin.com.

CAST OF CHARACTERS

Dev Wyatt—Former police officer who suffered major injuries at the hands of his father that led to him leaving the force. Now works as a rancher at Reaves ranch, which has been in his grandmother's family for generations.

Sarah Knight—Rancher helping her father run their ranch next door to the Reaves ranch. Lifelong friends with Dev Wyatt, she convinces him to be the father of her baby with the understanding he won't be involved in the baby's life.

Duke Knight—Owner of the Knight ranch. Sarah's adoptive father. Rachel's biological father. Cecilia's uncle. Foster father to Liza, Nina, Cecilia and Felicity.

Pauline Reaves—Grandmother to the Wyatt brothers.

Anth Wyatt—Man behind the threatening notes being left for the Wyatt brothers.

Jamison, Cody, Brady, Gage Wyatt—Dev's brothers, who all work in various law enforcement capacities and are being threatened by the same man.

Liza, Nina, Felicity, Cecilia and Rachel—Sarah's adoptive/foster sisters, all involved with their own Wyatt brother.

Prologue

"You're avoiding me."

Dev Wyatt looked up from the beer in his hand to the woman he was indeed avoiding at all costs. He didn't know if she meant tonight at his brother's and her foster sister's wedding or in general, because both were true.

But he was *especially* avoiding her tonight because she was wearing a dress that made what he had been trying to ignore for years all too clear. Sarah Knight was hot and he had no business noticing the generous curves all too invitingly showcased in some silky siren-red fabric.

Worse, he had no business considering her... proposition. Even though it had been lodged in his head for the entire month she'd been hounding him over it. She was his neighbor, adopted daughter of the man he looked up most to in the world, a good eight years younger than him, *and* a business partner of sorts. With neighboring ranches, and their siblings losing their minds and all marrying each other, they helped each other quite a bit.

He took a swig of beer then scowled at her. "Of course I'm avoiding you, Sarah. You've lost your mind and I'm tired of you trying to drag me into it."

He didn't have to look at her to know she would have raised her chin at that.

"It isn't losing my mind to go after what I want," she said stubbornly. And worse, resolutely. Even his hard head had nothing on Sarah's resolute.

She wanted a baby. Dev couldn't figure out why. She was only twenty-five. She wasn't exactly running out of time for the whole husband and kids thing.

When he'd brought that up, she'd scoffed.

I'm never going to find someone. I don't leave my ranch, and I don't want to. But I do want to be a mother. I've given it a lot of thought and you are the best option for father.

He'd given her every argument he could think of. Sperm bank? Too expensive. Adoption? She herself was adopted and wanted someone in her life to be genetically related to her. Stranger at a bar? Similar reasons to the adoption and worse, what if the stranger wanted to be involved?

He'd tried them all, and she had rational, reasonable responses to every excuse he put up. Not that having sex with him to get a baby was in any way rational or reasonable to begin with.

"You're young," Dev insisted. "You might change your mind." He nodded out to where his brother Brady was dancing with his new wife, Cecilia. He never would have predicted that. Things and people changed. "You might want all that in a few years."

Sarah looked at Cecilia and Brady smiling at each other. She seemed to give that some thought, but he should have known better. She turned her big blue eyes on him.

"Are you going to change your mind about not wanting a family? Are you going to change your mind about running Reaves Ranch?"

He could lie and say a person never knew what might change, but no. Those were the two tenets of his life—keeping everyone at arm's length and running his grandmother's ranch, which had been in his family for generations. Something *good* his blood had done with this earth.

Sarah knew it just as well as he did, so he said nothing.

But she nodded as if he'd agreed with her. "And I'm not going to change my mind about wanting to be a mother, and not really wanting a partner to do it. You're the only guy I know who doesn't want a family and isn't going to change his mind, but who I know well enough to…you know. So I'm not letting this go. Might as well give in."

The worst part was knowing that when Sarah got an idea in her head, she did *not* let it go. He'd have to keep fending her off for…forever.

She touched his arm so he had to look down at her. Sarah was usually all sharp edges and sharper words, but her expression was open and vulnerable here. Which was *horrifying*.

"You're the only one who can help me, Dev. Please."

Dev couldn't remember Sarah ever saying please to him, or worse, asking him for anything. No one asked him for anything anymore. Ever since he'd barely survived his father's attack on him over a decade ago, leaving him permanently damaged—body and spirit—the best he could hope for was ranching. For being considered the grumpy Wyatt brother, whose only use was keeping an eye on Grandma Pauline. Not that she needed any tending.

Sarah wanted to get pregnant and raise a baby on her own, with no one knowing he was the father. Which didn't bother him because he didn't want to be a father or a husband. He had plans to be alone for the rest of his life.

Still, she was asking him to…sleep with her. Maybe the reasons were biological. The act was *personal*, though.

It was wrong, but she was looking up at him, blue eyes sincere rather than piercing daggers like usual. Her touch was light instead of the random punches she usually aimed at him if she was going to touch him.

Because Sarah was the only one in his life who rarely treated him like he was fragile. Enough that she was asking him for this. She thought he could do it. Give her this thing she so desperately wanted that she'd been bugging him about it for weeks. Hounding him and refusing to find another alternative. Because she wanted it this way.

And she needed him.

No one should need him, and he shouldn't fool himself into thinking he could help. Not anymore.

He tried to fight the overwhelming need to give in. Maybe Sarah knew what she wanted, but she didn't know what she was *asking*. She couldn't want help from him. No one could.

"Dev. Just once." She slid her hand up his arm, and of all the ways she'd touched him in the twenty-some years he'd lived with his grandmother at Reaves Ranch with Sarah next door at Knight Ranch, she'd never once touched him like *that*. "If it doesn't work," she continued, leaning in so that her painted mouth was all too close to his, "I'll let it go. Promise."

He'd be stupid to believe her. She'd never let it go. And just once would be…well, something like a catastrophe.

Aren't you intimately acquainted with catastrophe?

He downed his beer. He couldn't do it. He couldn't. But he had a very bad feeling he was going to end up doing it, one way or another.

"Better drink up," he muttered, heading for the bar.

SARAH WOKE UP the next morning with a pounding headache, and only fuzzy memories of Dev in her hotel room. Much as it had been her idea, and she'd relentlessly hounded Dev until he'd given in, she'd still been more than a little nervous to have sex with someone she'd known her whole life. With the sole purpose of getting pregnant. So getting *really* drunk had been an excellent plan.

She even applauded herself for it as weeks passed. That's what she'd wanted. The act that led to a baby, not the act that *meant* something. She tried not to think of the night that was just fuzzy memories of a few kisses and touches and laughing a little *too* hard at Dev Wyatt kissing her.

When she did think about it, she was glad for the lack of memory. She couldn't remember what Dev looked like naked, which was good considering how closely they worked together on their neighboring ranches. Sometimes she wasn't even sure they'd actually *done* anything, considering how Dev didn't treat her any differently as the weeks piled up. Maybe he'd just let her think they had.

Or maybe her plan had worked.

From that morning after, she'd counted down the days until the earliest moment she could take a pregnancy test. Now she just had to pray that one drunk hookup with one of her best friends in the world had yielded what she'd always wanted.

A baby.

She inhaled sharply. Today was the day. She'd driven two towns over to buy the pregnancy test. In the Walmart bathroom, she'd discovered that her insane plan had indeed worked.

She was pregnant. The test in her hand said so.

It didn't feel real. She'd expected to be magically transformed. Her plan had worked. There were still a hell of a lot more steps to go: a doctor's appointment, lying to her family that she'd hooked up with a random stranger, and then actually preparing for a baby. But she'd expected to feel settled and ready once she'd seen the positive result.

She was thrilled. Ecstatic. But…was there *really* a baby in there? She hadn't had any noticeable symptoms. She'd overanalyzed every cramp, every moment of tiredness, and determined that nothing was all that different.

Maybe the test was wrong. She went through the whole process over again, with the same result. She threw everything away, washed her hands and then headed out of the store to her truck.

She was going to believe she'd succeeded. She was pregnant. Maybe she didn't feel different yet, but she would. As she went through everything she had to do, she'd have more and more belief, until there was a little baby in her arms.

Her own baby. Someone who shared her blood. Someone she'd be able to look at and maybe see her own eyes or nose. A mix of her and…

Dev.

She couldn't tell anyone else yet, but she could tell him. She drove back home, deciding she'd stop by the Reaves ranch.

She wanted a baby for herself. Someone to belong to her. Her sisters were all off married or living with their Wyatt boyfriends. The Knight house was quiet with just her and Dad. Much as Sarah loved her adopted father—the only father she could remember—she wanted more than just…the two of them.

She wanted to be a mother. She wanted a child.

The plan had been a little far-fetched but it had given her exactly what she wanted—what she needed.

It was all about her. She convinced herself of that over and over again. Until she parked her car next to the barn on the Reaves Ranch.

She walked inside. Dev was brushing down his horse, that permanent scowl affixed to his face. He said it was just his expression, but Sarah knew it was pain. After a long day of riding, his leg hurt him.

She stood in the doorway of the barn and admitted that as much as she'd done this for her own self, she'd also harbored a tiny hope that the reality of a baby might…reach Dev. He was a good man—as good as his brothers. The problem was, since his injuries had kept him from returning to law enforcement, he considered himself less than those brothers.

He wasn't, but he'd have to come to that conclusion on his own.

So if a baby woke him up out of the dark cloud he kept himself in, that would be icing on the cake. She wouldn't *expect* it, but she could *hope* for it.

"Help you?" he demanded when she thought she'd been staring unnoticed.

Still, she didn't startle. She was too used to his grumpy preternatural observations. So she stepped forward. The faint light of the barn highlighted him, and his face looked…hard. There was something edgy and dangerous about him in this light.

It gave her an odd shiver of foreboding, but she pushed that away. She came up to stand next to him. "Well, it worked. The whole baby thing."

He looked down at her, expression guarded. "Congratulations," he said, with absolutely no inflection on the word.

"Thank you. It's early yet, and I'll have to go to the doctor, but…" She felt teary, surprisingly emotional over telling him. But it was big. Huge. "Thank you, Dev. I don't think I could ever tell you how much it means to me that—"

"Don't mention it. Ever. Really."

He didn't ask her anything else, but he gave her a brush and they worked in companionable silence. It felt…right. He'd given her what she'd always wanted, and now things would go back to normal.

Until she had to tell her family. Until she started to show. Until she had a baby.

She laughed and shook her head. Life was about to get flipped on its head, and that was fine. That was what she wanted. But there was more to this than what she wanted. Something she hadn't predicted. "If you ever want to—"

"I don't," he said, and there was more emotion in those two words than everything he'd said so far.

"Okay, I'm only saying it because you're alone, Dev. Not because I need you to be involved. You're just the only one who…" She trailed off. It seemed cruel to point out all their siblings were building lives, she was having a baby and Dev was still…in a black cloud of his own making.

"I'm exactly where I have to be," Dev replied. He took the brush from her and tossed it in a pail. "I'm heading inside for dinner. I'm sure Grandma Pauline made enough." Then he walked away with that kind-of invitation hanging there.

Sarah could only frown after him, mulling over what he'd said. Because *have* to be wasn't the same as *want* to be.

Chapter One

In June, Sarah had broken the news to her family. She'd refused to name the father no matter how they'd prodded. From there, she'd begun to adjust to her new normal. It wasn't all that different than her old one.

If she lived with the tiny hope Dev might slowly come around, she didn't let on to that expectation to him or anyone else. She kept it buried deep.

In August, she'd found out she was having a boy. While her sisters all had girls, *she* was going to have a boy. Much as she would have been happy with any healthy child, a boy was a relief. Sarah wouldn't know what to do with a girl. She barely knew what to do with herself when it came to all the girly things her sisters seemed so natural at.

Now, as November rolled on toward Christmas, she was having to come to grips with the reality of being a very pregnant woman on an isolated ranch during a severe, unpredictable winter.

She would say Dev didn't act any differently toward her—they still argued and bickered. He was annoyingly high-handed about decisions that affected both ranches. But he sneakily kept her from over-taxing herself, especially in these later months, and he had a way of watching her that made goose bumps pop up on her arms and had her casting back for any dim memory of that night.

She reminded herself, almost daily, that she had gotten exactly what she'd wanted, and any linger-ing weirdness she sensed was both a figment of her imagination and something that would disappear once the baby was born.

Baby boy Knight was due on Christmas Day, and Sarah liked the idea of it. He'd always have a birth-day full of family, no matter how far-flung they may all be.

She still hadn't figured out a name. She could name him Evan after her late adopted mother, Eva. Evan Knight. It might work.

There was always DJ. She couldn't help but laugh-ing at the image of telling Dev she was going to name the baby Devin Junior. His horror would be epic. But it could also be an homage to her father. Duke Knight.

There were so many options. She pulled her scarf up over her mouth as she walked from her truck to the barn where she knew Dev would be mucking out the stalls. It was a frigid cold winter already, and every day seemed to dig deeper into the subzero tempera-tures. Inside, Sarah was an overheated mess of giant pregnant belly, so the cold felt good.

She walked into the stables, knowing Dev would kick her right back out. She'd needed the walk, the fresh air. A few moments alone, and then spending some time with someone who wouldn't fuss.

He'd tell her to go away, or to sit down, but he wouldn't flutter about like her father and sisters did. She stepped into the building, immediately smiling at the smell of hay and manure. Home.

"You aren't supposed to be here," Dev said without turning around.

"Why not?"

"No mucking. No overexerting yourself. Isn't that what your doctor said after your last checkup?"

Sarah wrinkled her nose. Her blood pressure had been a little high and she'd been having some mild on-and-off contractions. She was supposed to "take it easy" and it was driving her insane.

"I'm bored to death. Women on the prairie—"

"Spare me a lecture about women on the prairie and sit your butt down," Dev muttered irritably, never breaking his mucking stride. "There's plenty of paperwork to do."

"God help me."

Still, she sat down. Because the baby had begun to kick. She could feel the press of either his heel or knee against her belly. She loved feeling the shape of him through her stomach, the roll and kicks. Even the hiccups.

She looked up to find Dev watching her. He did that more and more as her body bloomed. She hadn't pressed him on becoming more involved. That wouldn't work with Dev. She just held on to that hope.

She pushed herself back up to her feet and waved him over. "Come here."

"Why?" he asked suspiciously.

"Because I'm fat and miserable. Come over here."

Reluctantly, he moved to her. She grabbed his hand and placed it over her stomach, under her coat but over her sweater.

He made a pained face, like she was forcing him to pet a snake. But what he could hide on his face, he couldn't hide in his voice. "That feels like a foot," he said, full of awe.

"Doesn't it?" She kept pressing his hand right there, following the rolling movement of the foot across her side. "He can kick like the devil, right up here in my ribs. He's going to be a hell of a rider. I can tell."

Dev shook his head. "You can't tell," he muttered, but he didn't take his hand away.

She let the moment stretch out, and even knowing what his reaction could be, she felt like she had to offer it again. "Dev... Just so you know. If you ever want—"

"I don't."

Well, she supposed that was that.

"Let's go get some breakfast."

She forced a smile. "It's almost like you knew I came over here to have Grandma Pauline ply me with biscuits and gravy."

He made a noncommittal noise as he limped for the door. Winter made his limp worse, which meant his pain was worse. Sarah wished there was some way to help him. Usually she took over chores this time of year—snuck in before he could get to them. One week last December she'd had to get up at three in the morning every day to beat him, but she'd done it.

None of that this winter, only sympathy and a weird twist of guilt that was totally out of place.

She followed him outside and toward the house. Dev's truck was parked in front of it, at an odd angle.

"You lose a tire?"

Dev stopped short, studied his truck and shook his head at the way it listed to one side. "Not that I knew of."

She followed him closer to the truck, but her heart started beating hard in her ears as she realized the cause of the flat tire.

A knife was sticking out of the rubber, a note attached.

It's Not Over was written in big thick black letters. Underneath were two letters. AW. Ace Wyatt.

Sarah could scarcely catch her breath. It couldn't be. Ace Wyatt was dead. It had to be a mistake. She looked to Dev for some kind of reassurance, but he stood so preternaturally still, there was no comfort to be found.

DEV STARED AT the words. The letters. He'd forgotten Sarah behind him. Forgotten the world around him entirely. For a few awful seconds he was back in the Badlands with his father.

It'll never be over, Devin.

"It can't be Ace." Sarah's voice was shrill behind him. "He's dead. You all made sure. He's dead."

Dev came back to the present, to the reality. "We identified his body," he said, his voice an awful rasp even to his own ears.

"And Jamison had those tests done. He made sure it was Ace."

Dev sucked in a breath. Sarah was right. Even though he'd seen Ace's lifeless body in the morgue himself, it was so easy to believe he was some kind of…evil spirit. But Sarah's reminder grounded him to reality. They'd seen him. They'd tested the body to make sure.

Ace was dead. The father who'd tortured them as children in his dangerous biker gang, then made their adulthoods as much hell as he could, was gone.

But there was an AW from his past who wasn't.

"You have to—"

Before Sarah could tell him what he had to do, the sound of an engine interrupted the quiet of the morning. Faint at first, but growing louder until Jamison's truck appeared on the rise.

Sarah let out an audible whoosh of breath, but Dev didn't match her relief. She was happy Jamison was here to take care of things, but if Jamison was here this early, it could only mean he'd gotten a similar threat.

When Dev realized Cody was in the passenger seat, his dread dug even deeper. The secret he'd kept, no matter how guilty it had made him feel for a decade now, was showing up on his doorstep in the worst possible way.

A threat to his brothers.

They got out of the truck—his oldest and youngest brothers, respectively. Both lived out in Bonesteel with their wives and children. For Jamison that meant his wife, Liza, and her young half sister, Gigi. For Cody that meant his high-school sweetheart, Nina, eight-year-old daughter, Brianna, and a baby on the way.

Just like you.

Except he did everything in his power not to think about Sarah's baby as anything close to his. Because Sarah's baby wasn't his. It was a favor he'd done her at only a slight cost to himself. Mainly, his sanity. There couldn't even be that cost now. That secret was even more paramount than the one he'd carried since his father had injured him irrevocably.

Jamison and Cody wore matching grim expressions as they walked toward him and Sarah.

"I see you got the same message we did," Cody said, nodding toward the tire.

Dev pointed at Jamison's truck. "Quick fix."

Jamison shook his head. "Mine was on the door to my office at city hall. Along with a machete."

"Mine was wrapped around a brick that went through my storefront window," Cody said with an even tone, though fury was stamped across his features.

"Gage had an arrow through his patrol car window, Brady had a dead animal on the porch with the note, and Tucker's was on his porch as well—sticking out of a charred, headless doll," Jamison continued, using that emotionless cop voice that usually grated on Dev's nerves.

This morning he found it oddly reassuring.

"The notes all said the same thing," Cody continued, as if the image of a charred, headless doll didn't bother him.

"It can't be Ace," Sarah said, her voice an octave too high. Dev had forgotten about her there.

"You need to get inside," he said gruffly. It was cold and she was supposed to be taking it easy, not panicking in the frigid temperatures. He thought of the feeling of the baby's foot pushing against her stomach. A real, living, thriving human being.

He couldn't think about any of that.

"You will not order me inside, Dev Wyatt," she fumed.

"We'll all go inside," Jamison offered in a conciliatory tone, gesturing Sarah toward the house. "And you're right, it can't be Ace," he agreed as they all trudged toward the door of Grandma Pauline's house. Except for Cody, who was collecting the note and knife in evidence bags.

"We were too careful to doubt he's dead," Jamison was saying to Sarah as he held the door open for her.

"What else isn't over that has to do with all six of you, though?" Sarah asked.

Jamison and Sarah moved into the warmth of Grandma Pauline's kitchen, but warmth seemed all wrong. So Dev could only hesitate on the threshold, even as Cody came in behind him.

Grandma stood at the stove. She had a wooden spoon in one hand and her white hair was pulled back in a bun. Dev noticed the flash of worry in her gaze before she schooled it away into her usual take-no-prisoners demeanor.

"Well, what are the cavalry doing here?" she demanded.

Jamison and Cody gave her weak smiles. When Grandma saw Sarah she immediately grabbed her and had her in a chair with a plate of food in front of her before Dev could even move.

"You rest and eat," Grandma ordered Sarah. "You three can discuss your business elsewhere."

"No," Sarah argued through a mouth full of biscuit. "I have to hear this too. I think we all do."

"Tucker, Brady and Gage will all be here when they can. We want to compare notes," Cody said. "We all got threatening notes this morning." He held up the bag to Grandma Pauline, and she squinted to read.

Her mouth firmed, but she went back to stirring her gravy without another word.

"I talked to my friend at North Star on the way over," Cody said, referring to the secretive group he'd worked for to help take down their father's gang. "The Sons of the Badlands are weak, mostly disbanded, but that doesn't mean they're all gone or in jail. Any one of them could still harbor a grudge."

"Wouldn't they just hold that grudge against North Star?" Sarah asked.

"Not just. I think they'd hold a grudge against anyone they could. And North Star is a group of highly trained operatives. Hard to find, harder to pin down. We're a much easier target. We're the reason Ace was in jail when he was killed."

"But you're not the reason he's dead," Sarah argued.

"Depends on how in touch with reality you are. Ace's cronies often weren't. We'd be easy to blame. He doesn't get stabbed in jail if he's not there," Jamison said.

"But that wasn't all six of you," Sarah insisted. "You and Cody were the ones instrumental in getting him in jail."

"But Felicity and Gage were instrumental in the trial," Cody returned, speaking of their brother Gage and his wife, Felicity. "Which was what prompted Ace to be moved to the prison where he died. Brady too, for that matter."

"What about Dev? He hasn't done anything."

That might have felt like a stab if it were true. Unfortunately, it wasn't true at all. He'd done something no one was ever going to forgive him for.

He thought of the list Cody had gone through outside. All the different ways this message had been given to his brothers. All the ways they were now in danger. Maybe it wasn't because of him, but it didn't matter now. He had to tell them the truth.

And it would change everything.

"There's something I've never told you. Any of you." Dev heard nothing but a buzzing in his own ears. He didn't want to say the words. Didn't want to do any of this, but that AW was impossible to ignore.

And his brothers' lives were at stake…their families' lives. "Ace had another son. His name is Anth Wyatt. AW."

Chapter Two

Dev waited. For the questions, the demands, the accusations. He should have known better. All of those things he expected he could have met with cool detachment.

"Why didn't you tell us?" Jamison asked, his voice rough and…wrecked. Dev had never heard that tone from his brother no matter what had happened in their lives. And boy, had they survived some wreckage.

Dev swallowed down the emotion coating his throat. He fell back into the black void of detachment that had gotten him through those first months after he'd come out of the coma his father had beaten him into. "Anth is the only reason Ace didn't kill me back then," he managed to say, sounding flat and unaffected even though he was anything but. "In return, I made a promise. Which I'm now breaking by telling you he exists."

"You think it's him?" Cody asked. He'd recovered his voice more than Jamison.

"I don't know why, after all this time. But AW isn't some coincidence. You don't sign a note to us with

AW and not expect it to be Ace or someone connected to him." Ace was dead. They'd made sure of that.

But the effects of Ace would live on. Why had he been stupid enough to think they wouldn't?

Silence swallowed the kitchen whole. Dev wasn't sure he'd ever heard such a silence in this kitchen. There had been months of danger and fears last year, but someone had always had something to say.

Dev couldn't help but glance at Sarah. She sat at the table, eyes wide, mouth open, still holding onto a forkful of food that had never made it up to her mouth. Her belly was big and round and all he could think about was his hand on her belly—feeling the outline of that foot inside of her.

A foot they'd made together during a night that played over and over again in his mind when he didn't want it to.

Especially now.

He'd failed her. He'd believed it was over and let himself be stupid enough to think he could give someone something.

"I guess you should tell us everything you know about this Anth Wyatt," Cody said, finally breaking the heavy, choking silence. "Starting with..." Cody trailed off. That stoic demeanor he'd been trying to hold on to slipped, and he raked his hands through his hair. "I don't understand, Dev."

His brothers looked at him like he'd killed something in front of them. And he supposed he had. Their trust. So, what was there to understand? He was no upstanding Wyatt. He wouldn't say he was like his father—he wasn't an evil madman. He was like their mother—weak-willed enough to care more about self-preservation than any of his loved ones. The ones he should have protected.

Sarah got up from her seat and came to stand between him and his brothers. She laid her hand on his arm—gently like she had at Brady's wedding. Like Sarah had some well of *gentleness* she'd always hidden.

"I'm sure if we all sit down, Dev can tell us the whole story," Sarah said authoritatively, reminding him of Grandma Pauline. Until she tried to force a smile at him. "There's an explanation, of course."

"Not the one you're hoping for," he replied bleakly.

She swallowed at that, but she didn't drop her hand or flinch. She pointed him to the table, and Dev didn't know what else to do but sit.

His brothers did too, on the opposite side of the table from him and Sarah. Grandma Pauline piled plates with food and set them in front of each of her grandsons. She still hadn't said anything.

When had Grandma Pauline ever not said anything?

Dev could only stare at his plate, words tumbling around in his brain, but none of them making it to his mouth.

Sarah reached beneath the table and took his hand. He didn't know what to do with her faith in him, because God knew he was about to destroy it. But wasn't that what he needed to do? Just blow it all up, lay it all out there.

Because someone thought it wasn't over, and he knew who.

"It goes back to when Dad and I had our little standoff," Dev managed to say. He didn't sound so devoid of emotion now. The emotions all but strangled the words and they sounded like just that.

He wasn't sure he could do this with Sarah holding his hand. He wasn't sure he could do it without.

"You've never told us much about that," Cody said, with enough detachment Dev could only be jealous.

"What was there to tell? I thought I had him. I thought in a one-on-one fight I could take him down and arrest him. I didn't. He beat me within an inch of my life and then let me go." Dev tried to tug his hand away from Sarah's, but she held firm under the table. It was a curse and a relief. "The only part I left out was that someone else was there."

"This...other son?" Jamison supplied.

"I didn't know that at first, though he looked like Ace. More like Ace than we do, except he had blue eyes." Dev could remember all too well. He'd been cocky and stupid and had tried to take down his father on his own.

Then there'd been another Ace. Same face. Same build. Same sneer, but blue eyes instead of hazel.

"He stopped Ace. I was in and out. I don't remember much." He didn't tell his brothers the pain had been so bad he'd half wished to die. At least then it would be over. He'd been twenty-two and stupid. So damn stupid. "He gave Ace some song and dance about how killing your own son, even one as shameful as me, was a distraction from what Ace was meant to do. That it might even ruin his karmic reward or whatever Ace was always going on about. I'm not sure Ace was swayed so much as he paused to think."

Think about the ways he could torture his son so much better if he were alive—alive and unable to continue in law enforcement. Alive and the weakest link in the Wyatt brothers.

But that wasn't what they were talking about.

"Anth came over and told me his name. Told me we were brothers. He said if I wanted to live, if I wanted my family to live, I had to promise to never mention his existence to anyone. If I agreed, I'd survive. If I didn't, we'd all be dead."

The worst part in telling his brothers was he knew what they would have done. They would have accepted death. Better to die a noble one than lie for Ace.

"I promised," Dev managed to say, though it felt like being back in the Badlands, broken and bloody. Failing. "Next thing I knew I woke up in the hospital."

"Why didn't you tell us when Ace died? That there might still be someone out there who wanted to hurt us?"

"Anth didn't hurt me. He saved my life, what was left of it. I thought it was over. Whatever or whoever he was."

"But it's not," Jamison said flatly.

Dev thought of the notes they'd all gotten. No, the worst part wasn't knowing his brothers would have handled it differently. The worst part was knowing he wouldn't change a second of it if he could go back. Even knowing it'd come back to bite him. "No. No, it isn't over."

NO ONE HAD EATEN. Even Sarah hadn't been able to stomach more than a few bites. Despite everything that had happened last year as the Wyatts had navigated Ace and the Sons' constant attempts to hurt them, she had never seen everyone look so...wrecked.

No one was going to speak, and even though Sarah had no right, she couldn't stand this. "Well, I'm sure we're all glad you made the choice that kept you alive, Dev," she said, maybe a little too loudly and a little too pointedly at Jamison and Cody.

She was gratified to see Cody wince and Jamison close his eyes as if physically pained.

"She's right, Dev," Jamison said, opening his eyes and looking right at him. "You did what you had to do to survive. We understand that. It's... The notes are concerning, but we'd never blame you for doing what you had to."

Dev didn't say anything, just tried to tug his hand away from hers under the table again, but she wouldn't let him. She held on tight.

"Besides," Cody offered. "Now we know. Which means once Brady, Gage and Tucker get here, we can figure out a way to protect ourselves from this Anth Wyatt."

Dev looked down at his plate. Then, in a sudden move that finally freed his hand from hers, he scraped back from the table. "Got chores," he muttered. He stalked outside before anyone could stop him.

Sarah thought about letting him go. He needed some time to work through this, and Dev best worked through things alone. But he would convince himself he was in the wrong, and she couldn't let him do that.

She got to her feet, ready to follow, but both Jamison and Cody hurried to block the door. "This isn't about you, Sarah," Cody said.

She wanted to smack him, but instead she fixed him with her most imperious scowl—one she'd learned from watching Grandma Pauline for years. "You're right, this is about Dev. Believing he failed you somehow."

Jamison and Cody exchanged a glance as though that's exactly what Dev had done. Her fingers curled into fists, though she kept them at her sides.

"He did what he had to do to keep himself alive. If you blame him for that, for even a second, you're nothing but egotistical, self-centered blowhards who don't love your brother the way you should."

"I said we didn't blame him. Right here at this table. You heard me."

"Yeah, you said it. Now, why don't you work on believing it." She pushed between them and out into the mudroom, pulled her coat on, and then braved the outside.

Sarah knew there were only two reasons they'd let her leave without following. One, she was pregnant and they were all treating her with kid gloves, and two, because Grandma Pauline likely stepped in and stopped them.

She headed right for the stables and wasn't surprised to find Dev saddling up his horse. He didn't turn around, though she could tell he knew she was there by the slight pause in his movements.

"You want to yell at me, fine, but it'll have to wait until I've done the morning rounds."

"Yell at you?" Sarah could only stand in confusion as he cinched the saddle and started moving Roscoe toward the door.

"In fact, don't bother," he continued, as if she hadn't voiced any confusion. "I'm sorry. No amount of yelling is going to make me feel more sorry."

"Why would you feel sorry?"

For the first time he stopped moving. He held Roscoe's reins in his hand and looked at her like she was the one who wasn't making any sense. "If you'd known I'm sure you wouldn't have involved me in the whole…" He waved at her stomach with his free hand.

Sarah settled her hands over her bump. "You gave me exactly what I asked for. I don't know why you'd be sorry about that. And I really don't know why this would have changed my mind."

"Ace—"

"—is dead," Sarah said firmly, cutting him off. She stepped toward him and took his hand just as she had inside. She needed that anchor as much as she suspected he did. Because the thought of him so close to death… It had been bad enough those ten years ago when she'd been an emotional teenager and visited him in the hospital. Worse now knowing how…he'd survived it. All alone. "You said you had to do it."

"No," Dev said in that voice she remembered from that awful time. He'd spent weeks in the hospital after he'd finally woken up from the coma, but when he'd gotten home it hadn't been…good. Dev had been like a void. No emotions. No…personality. He'd been a shell. It had taken him years to come back to himself. He still wasn't all the way there, but this made it all worse again.

It about broke her heart.

"I said he saved my life on a condition. It's not the same as *having* to do it."

"It is to me," Sarah said quietly, afraid if she spoke any louder her voice and composure might break.

He shook his head. "Jamison never would have agreed to that deal. That I know for sure."

"And Jamison would be dead. That *I* know for sure. And if he'd died then, Liza and Gigi would probably be dead, too, since Jamison was the reason they escaped the Sons. Heck, maybe all of you would be dead after last year's troubles. So if this whole thing with Ace and his other son had to happen, then I'm damn glad it happened to you, who'd had the sense to make a deal."

He tugged his hand out of hers and she couldn't hold on to his grasp though she tried.

"A deal with the devil?"

"With the outcome that let you live." Since she couldn't hold on to his hand, she reached up and touched his face. She wasn't prone to physical acts of affection, but the thought of life and death had her feeling weepy and desperate. Or maybe that was pregnancy hormones. She'd happily blame it on that. "You being alive is the most important thing to me."

He covered her hand as if to pull it off his face, but she had a flash of a kiss, a murmur. The feelings of their bodies moving together. Something... otherworldly.

She blinked as he removed her hand and dropped it. Memory or fantasy, hard to tell. And pointless either way.

"Stop being nice to me," he muttered. "It's weird."

"It isn't weird when you're the—"

He cut her off with a look. Because she wasn't supposed to think of him as the father of her baby. Her baby didn't have a father in *that* sense, and she'd been okay with that. Grandma Pauline had raised those six grandsons of hers on her own. Turned them into amazing, wonderful men after terrible childhoods stuck in their father's gang. She'd wanted to do that, too.

Sometimes she just had a hard time remembering that. Which irritated her, though she wasn't even sure why or who she was irritated with. Him or herself.

"It's Christmastime," Sarah said loftily. "Peace on earth and goodwill toward men. I'm good-willing you. Get used to it." She winced as pain tightened her belly. Stupid early contractions.

Dev was immediately dropping his horse's reins and propelling her back and onto the rickety bench. "Damn it, Sarah."

"It's nothing," she said, breathing like the doctor had told her to. "The doctor said so."

"No, the doctor said you had to take it easy. Not that it was *nothing*."

"I *am* taking it easy." The pain eased, slowly, but it eased. She managed a smile up at him. "See? All gone. The doctor said the contractions should come and go for *weeks* without any progress. That is why I have an appointment every week until the due date. It's fine. I promise."

"Sarah." The stark way he said her name had the smile dying on her face as he kneeled before her.

"This is bad. It's danger all over again, and one we have less experience with. It's even more imperative that no one ever suspect…" There was a twist of pain on his face as he looked at her belly—a kind of pain she'd never seen him allow to show on his face like that. This time it was him grabbing her hands. "You need to stay away," he said resolutely. "Stay on your property. I'll keep helping out at your ranch for you, but you need to stay away. Stay in bed. Rest, like the doctor said. Please. I'm begging you."

She swallowed the lump in her throat. She didn't know how to do what he was asking, but she also didn't know how to say no to him when he was like this. Emotional and very close to desperate.

No, she couldn't argue with him. "I'll…try," she promised.

Chapter Three

Sarah spent the morning away from Dev and the Reaves ranch. She took some time off her feet until the contractions were completely gone. People might think she pushed herself too hard, but she was careful.

Besides, she was only two weeks away from her due date. What would be the harm in the baby coming now? She'd happily bake him a little longer, but labor wouldn't be the worst thing at this point. Especially on a day when there was no snow in the forecast.

Once she'd felt better and eaten some lunch, she'd bundled up and headed outside. Dev's dogs, which he'd insisted on having live at the Knight Ranch since the trouble last year, pranced ahead of her.

Staying inside made her too antsy and anxious and today, it made her replay Dev's emotional plea over and over in her head.

I'm begging you.

She couldn't…sit with that. She needed a chore to do, even if it wasn't labor intensive. She needed the cold winter air and something to do with her hands. She needed the ranch. It had always been her solace, her heart. No one could stop her from seeking that out just because she was going to have a baby soon.

She smoothed her hands over her belly—even bulkier with the heavy coat on over it. She'd give her baby the space to like and love whatever he wanted, but that didn't mean she couldn't fantasize about him feeling the same way about the Knight Ranch as she did.

What about Reaves Ranch?

She looked to the west. Dev was the only Wyatt brother who'd shown an actual interest in Grandma Pauline's ranch. If he didn't have any kids, what would happen to it? Would the Reaves Ranch be sold off to a stranger?

She shook her head as if to shake the thoughts away. There would be many, many years of Dev and Grandma Pauline inhabiting this earth before she had to worry about that. Maybe her baby was technically a Wyatt, but right now Dev didn't want to acknowledge that.

Not just for his own reasons anymore, but for safety. Because Anth Wyatt apparently existed and was threatening all six brothers.

It made her want to cry. This was supposed to be over—the shadow of Ace Wyatt on their lives gone. Instead, just as they'd settled into this new normal… here was another facet of Ace haunting them.

Would that always be the case?

She knew that was bothering Dev, likely his brothers too. That horrible feeling they'd never be free of Ace even in death. And it wasn't just them—they'd all married or were in the process of marrying her sisters. Making families of their own.

Wyatts and her sisters pairing up wasn't a great thing to dwell on with her hands on her stomach, where Dev's child grew. She marched forward. Maybe she couldn't muck stalls, ride a horse or even go around breaking up ice in the troughs, but she could tidy the tools or do a little light sweeping or *something*.

But before she could make it to the stables, Duke pulled up next to her in his truck. She knew he'd been out checking fence lines to make sure they were strong enough to survive any winter storm that blew through.

He put the truck into Park and got out. "What do you think you're doing wandering around in this cold?"

She smiled at her father. He was a good man, even if he'd kept his share of secrets from them. He did what was right, and he was fiercely protective of his daughters—biological, adopted or fostered.

"I'm just antsy. I'm being careful. Promise."

He made a noise that was neither belief nor acceptance. Simple acknowledgment she'd spoken and he'd heard it. "Where were you this morning?"

Sarah wouldn't let herself fidget even though it felt a bit like an accusation. "Let Grandma Pauline feed me."

Duke studied her, clearly not believing that was the only reason she'd gone over there. Instead of lecturing her more, he reached out and squeezed her shoulder.

"Sarah, I hope you know what a joy you've been to me. Not just because you love the ranch like I do, but because you're a fine young woman with a good head on her shoulders."

Sarah blinked. Duke was the best dad in the world as far as she was concerned, but he wasn't big on emotional heart-to-hearts. Thank God. She didn't know what to do with...this. "Well, thanks."

"I may not be thrilled about the circumstances, but I'll support you and my grandchild any way I can."

"I... I know." She'd always known that, even if him saying it had a lump forming in her throat.

"Which is why I feel like it's pretty important to tell you something, and usually when I tell you something you get that hard head on and do the opposite. So I need you to promise me you'll listen."

Sarah wrinkled her nose. "You fight dirty."

"You're darn right," he said, smiling at her, his big hand still on her shoulder. Because he was always there.

"I don't know that I can promise outright, but I can promise to try not to be contrary for the sake of it."

Duke chuckled softly. "Well, I suppose that's about all I can ask." Then he sighed, almost sadly, as if the words weighed him down and were far more serious than she wanted to deal with when she was worried about Dev and this new danger.

Which she should probably tell Dad about.

Dad grabbed her other shoulder, gave her a gentle squeeze and met her gaze with his steady one. "Sarah, you can't save that boy. He has to save himself."

That simple statement hit its mark—a mark she hadn't realized she had. She wasn't trying to save Dev… She was just trying to…to… "I'm not trying to save anyone," she insisted, though of course she couldn't believe it now that she'd felt the weight of how right Duke was.

Duke gave her a pointed look. "Baby girl, you have been poking that boy back into the living since the day he got home from the hospital. And you've done a good job. He wouldn't be where he is without you. But the rest of that journey is his to make."

She thought about Dev's blankness in the kitchen when he'd recounted Anth Wyatt to his brothers. How could emotional healing be his to do when he could simply shut down like that?

"I haven't heard the details yet, but if everyone's descending on Grandma Pauline's tonight, sounds like more trouble is brewing," Duke continued. "I don't want you involved. You've got to take it easy for that baby. I want you to stay away from the Wyatts for a while. Including tonight's dinner."

The knee-jerk emotions that had plagued her this entire pregnancy sprung to life, and she had to fight to keep the tears out of her eyes. "They're my family. And yours."

"Of course they are. I'm not saying it's their fault they've got trouble again. I'm not saying we should all hide and run away. I'm saying *you* need to stay away from it in your condition."

Dev had said the same thing, of course. She understood why, but that didn't mean she needed to be hidden away. "If there's trouble, I doubt me staying home by myself is—"

"Liza will come here with the girls. You two will babysit."

Sarah scowled. "While the menfolk have their grown-up conversation."

Duke sighed. "With four out of your five sisters. Come on now, girl. You have a baby to care about."

She put her hands protectively over her belly. "Caring about this baby doesn't mean I don't care about the safety of everyone I love. If some long-lost half brother is after them, it's not just them. It's *my* sisters too and—"

Duke's hands tightened on her shoulders.

"What did you say?" he demanded, suddenly fierce.

Sarah blinked at the sudden change in his demeanor. Had he not thought the dinner was as serious as that? "They got notes. All the brothers. From one of Ace's sons they didn't know about." She didn't add the part about Dev knowing. Didn't need to get into—

"I have to go." Duke released her abruptly and was immediately striding for his truck.

"Wha—"

"Liza will be over in a bit. You stay put, now." He got in the truck, pointed at her like she was a little girl again. "I mean it." The dogs sat on their butts as if he'd been talking to them.

Then he drove off, and Sarah stood in the stark winter afternoon wondering what on earth had gotten into everyone.

IT WASN'T ANY easier telling the truth to the rest of his brothers. Jamison was the oldest, the one who'd saved them all from the Sons, the one Dev had idolized before he'd ended up broken—so Dev had assumed that would be the worst. Letting down the person you most wanted to make proud.

The others were younger than him. They hadn't spent as much time in the Sons as he and Jamison had. They didn't fully...

But of course they did. Ace had kept Cody's wife on the run, resulting in his daughter being a secret from him for seven years. Ace had almost killed Gage last summer and had been instrumental in Felicity's own biological father hurting her. Ace had been in the periphery of Tucker and Brady's troubles this summer—but he'd been there. The reason. Always.

"It didn't occur to you to tell us once Ace was dead?" Brady said, his expression cop-blank and his voice grim.

"No. I thought it was over. Just like you."

"Clearly it's not."

"Clearly," Dev echoed.

"I'm still not following," Gage said. Usually the most easygoing brother, or at least the one more likely to tell a joke, there was nothing remotely light about Gage right now. "This Anth guy saved you?"

"He said he would make sure I didn't die if I promised to never tell anyone about his existence. I figured it was some kind of...conscience or whatever. We all have one. Why wouldn't this... Wyatt?" Which of course had an easy answer. Ace was always the why.

"And you don't have any idea who his mother is?"

Dev shook his head. "We didn't have much time for a heart-to-heart."

"After. You didn't even think to tell us?"

"I was a little busy, you know, recovering from a coma and learning how to walk again." Dev knew it was wrong to snap at his brothers. Their questions were valid, necessary even. "In the moment, I would have agreed to just about anything. After... Well, he'd held up his end of the bargain. Clearly he knew who I was, if not all of us. If he wanted to be a part of us, he could have been."

"Clearly he didn't want to be."

"Regardless, I'm alive, aren't I? I certainly don't know how. Ace wanted to kill me that day. None of this 'you're my progeny' stuff like he had with Jamison and Gage. He wanted me to be the lesson to all of you. So, whatever Anth did—I'm alive because of it. At the time, telling you guaranteed that I'd be bringing Ace back to our doorstep."

"He could have been behind any of what happened last year," Jamison said. "Framing Felicity for murder, everything that went down in the Badlands with Brady and Cecilia."

Dev was still struggling to deal with how utterly *destroyed* Jamison sounded. As if it was a personal betrayal he'd never get over. Because Jamison couldn't imagine it. Dev knew Jamison was good through and through, and he would have rather died than make a deal.

Just like then, Dev couldn't live up to Jamison's

perfect example. "He wasn't behind any of it though, was he?"

"That we know of," Jamison said softly.

No matter how soft, the truth of that was like a knife to the heart. Obviously he'd considered Anth might have something to do with all the danger that had befallen them last year. How could he not consider it? But there'd never been any evidence pointing to someone other than Ace or one of his Sons of the Badlands cronies.

But you didn't have to be the perpetrator of something to be involved. Ace had escaped connection with who knew how many crimes.

Duke burst into the kitchen, looking a little wild as all the brothers turned to him.

"What is it? Is something wrong?" Dev demanded, thoughts immediately going to Sarah and those contractions this morning.

"Tell me what's going on," Duke said, a little out of breath. "You were threatened."

"Duke, I can't tell you not to worry when there's a threat against us and your girls are involved, but it's being taken care of," Jamison said calmly, none of that hurt in his tone like it was when he spoke to Dev.

"Don't take that high-handed tone with me. Not only are all my daughters in the crosshairs here, but... Tell me about this son of Ace's."

All Dev's brothers turned to him. Because Anth Wyatt was his cross to bear. "I don't know much about him. Anth Wyatt spared my life back when Ace wanted to kill me. I don't have the slightest clue why he'd be threatening the six of us now, but I think it's him."

"He could have others," Tucker offered—speaking for the first time. "If Ace had one son with another woman, there could be more than one."

Duke scraped his hands over his face. "Could be, it's true, but this one…this Anth…" Duke trailed off on a pained breath.

"You know something about him?" Jamison asked.

"Not exactly. But I know who his mother is."

"How?"

Duke's expression was so grim, and the eye contact he made was with Dev and Dev alone. "Sarah's mother. Biological mother. She'd had a son with Ace, which was why Sarah's father asked Eva and me to take her. They were scared for her safety. Not because of Ace. Because of the son. Anth Wyatt."

Chapter Four

"I don't need babysitting."

Liza cooed at their niece, Felicity and Gage's sweet little Claire who was quickly creeping toward her first birthday. It would have been a nice moment. Hanging out with just Liza and the girls. Liza had six-year-old Gigi, technically her half sister, but Liza and Jamison were her guardians with her parents dead. Cody and Nina's eldest daughter Brianna and Gigi were good friends and were occupying each other upstairs.

"You can't be alone this close to your due date. Besides, Jamison already filled me in on what they're covering over at the ranch."

"What about *me*?"

"Your job is baby-growing and, soon enough, baby-pushing into the world. That's the big stuff, Sarah." Liza smiled reassuringly, but there was something all wrong about everything. The way Duke had taken off, the way Liza refused to talk about Anth Wyatt.

"Nina's pregnant," Sarah pointed out petulantly.

"She's five months pregnant and not having contractions on and off," Liza returned equitably.

"What's going on over there? I know about the mysterious brother, but…" She couldn't put her finger on the *wrong* feeling that kept crawling up her spine. Ever since Duke had taken off.

When Liza turned her back to Sarah, making a big fuss over putting Claire in her travel crib, Sarah's dread sank deeper.

"Liza, what is going on?"

Liza took a deep breath and let it out. She came back to Sarah, kneeling in front of where Sarah sat on what was usually Duke's recliner but she'd commandeered during this last month of her pregnancy.

"We all want you to take care of yourself," Liza said, patting Sarah's knee. "Contractions are nothing to mess around with."

"I wasn't even dilated. The doctor told me what to do and I have an appointment every week. Baby is pretty much all baked in there. The worry is over the top, unless there is something bigger at work here."

Liza started to shake her head, but Sarah pressed.

"Explain to me how knowing there's danger, but no one will tell me exactly what, is supposed to give me a calm, relaxing last few weeks of pregnancy?"

Brianna thundered down the stairs from where she and Gigi had been playing dolls. She slid into the living room in her usual boisterous fashion. "Aunt Sarah, can I feel your baby?" Brianna asked. Eight year old Brianna had been fascinated with Sarah's pregnancy ever since finding out her own mom was pregnant.

Sarah nodded and motioned her over. She took Brianna's hands and placed them on her stomach. "He's not moving around much right now, but you never know when he'll start kicking up a storm."

Gigi had followed and was peering down into Claire's crib, making funny faces at the baby who squealed in appreciative laughter.

Sarah wished she could enjoy it. Her nieces, her sister. Liza had only lived with the Knights a couple years after she'd escaped the Sons of the Badlands with Jamison when she'd been a teenager. Then she'd run away to go back into the gang and keep her sister safe. But Sarah had always looked up to her. She'd missed her when she'd left, been so angry at her for disappearing, but the past year and a half had done a lot to heal those hurts.

Liza was still that oldest sister who seemed to know how to hold everything together. After the girls got tired of baby watch, they moved to TV, and Claire dozed in her crib. Liza forced Sarah to eat dinner on the chair, fussing over her as if she was an invalid.

If it had been any other night, Sarah might have been able to relax and enjoy it, but worry kept her tense and frustrated.

Liza returned from the kitchen with a brownie, and Sarah took it eagerly as Liza perched on the arm of the chair and ate her own.

"Are you ever going to tell us who the father is?" Liza asked, quiet enough that the girls wouldn't hear as they watched their show.

Sarah shifted uncomfortably—both emotionally and physically. "It doesn't matter. Wouldn't you have rather lived a life without your father? Gigi's okay now, but wouldn't she have been better off if her mother had been able to get her away from your father?"

Liza pressed her lips together. "You're not doing this alone, because you have all us, but there is something to be said for a partner. I know you can do this, but I don't want you to close yourself off to possibilities."

Brownie finished, Sarah placed her hands firmly on her belly. "The only possibility I want is holding my son and raising him here. I'm not closing myself off to a partnership. I just know that everything I want is right here."

"Here. On this ranch with Duke. Getting a whole heck of a lot of help from Dev."

"We're neighbors. That's what ranching neighbors do. Help each other out. Especially when we're practically family what with the way you lot have off and married Wyatts."

"You two have an interesting relationship."

Sarah scooted down in the armchair. She had a bad feeling she knew where Liza was going, but she wasn't going to play along. "Interesting. Antagonistic. Potato potahto."

"You're a unit. You have been for quite some time. You work together. You have your own weird language. Dev's a tough nut to crack, but you seem to have cracked it on occasion."

Sarah snorted. "I wouldn't go that far."

"I know you, Sarah. You get plans and you go about enacting them without letting anyone know what you're doing. You have ideas that you keep to yourself but make happen through sheer force of will. I'm not saying I wouldn't bet on you if it came to it, but betting on Dev is…well, people are complicated."

Sarah fidgeted, her belly felt too weighted and her back was aching. Which was totally about pregnancy and not how Liza's words seemed to hit their mark. "I'm not betting on Dev."

Liza shrugged. "I don't believe you."

Before Sarah could get bent out of shape about that, Jamison came to collect Liza and Gigi, then Cody and Nina to pick up Brianna. They took Claire with them to drop back off at the Reaves Ranch since Felicity and Gage were staying with Grandma Pauline.

When Duke came in, he wasn't alone, and that scared Sarah to her bones. Dev was with him and they both looked at *her* with a grimness that could never be good.

DEV KNEW HE shouldn't have come. He should have let Duke handle this aspect of things. Duke would take care of his own. They'd all take care of each other. He didn't need to be smack dab in the middle of anything that involved Sarah.

But he'd found himself trailing after Duke anyway, and when Duke hadn't offered any objections, they'd driven over to the Knight house together.

Sarah eyed them both with mounting suspicion, her hands coming over her belly in a protective gesture. Something he refused to acknowledge twisted in Dev's gut.

"What is it?" she asked, her voice coming out strong even if the worry showed in her eyes.

"We're just going to move you over to Grandma Pauline's. Aside from Jamison and Cody's families in Bonesteel, everyone's going to be staying there, much as they can. Strength in numbers."

"What about you?" Sarah demanded, as Dev had known she would. Before Duke could give his lame excuses, Sarah continued. "If we're all going to be there, you should be, too."

"We've been trying to tell him that," Dev muttered, earning a glare from Duke.

"It's not necessary."

"Why not?" Sarah insisted.

"I'm not a part of this."

"Then neither am I," Sarah replied. "Not married to a Wyatt, and if working together on both ranches doesn't count for you, it doesn't count for me either. And if this is about me being pregnant—"

"It isn't," Dev said firmly. Again he got a glare from Duke. Maybe this was why he'd come though, because he knew she wouldn't get the unvarnished truth from anyone else. They'd try to dance around the problem—the danger.

He understood why. She was supposed to be relaxing and avoiding stress—but she had a connection to the man threatening them and it could not be ignored.

"Duke, you have to tell her. No amount of moving her and installing people around her is going to keep her safe if she doesn't know."

"Knew I shouldn't have let you come," Duke muttered.

"If someone doesn't tell me what I don't know right this second I am liable to go straight into labor. Spit it out."

Dev wished it was a much less scary a situation so he could find some enjoyment in how quickly Duke jumped to explain himself after that.

"I know a little about Anth Wyatt."

Sarah's eyebrows drew together. "More secrets?"

Dev winced at the hurt in her tone. Because this whole disaster was the unraveling of more secrets than he'd ever expected.

"I won't apologize for this secret. When your parents—"

"My parents!" she screeched, trying to push herself out of the chair, but Dev was quicker and was gently pressing his hand into her shoulder to keep her put.

"Let him finish," Dev ordered.

Sarah whipped a killing look up at him, but he nodded toward Duke.

"Your father was friends with Eva. From way back. We were friendly with your parents. They knew we had fostered girls. At that point we thought we couldn't have any children of our own." Duke rubbed a hand over his graying hair. "They came to us, a few weeks before you were born. Your mother had had a child from a previous relationship. They were afraid of both the man and the child. He'd been threatening your mother. They were worried about your safety.

They wanted someone to take you until they could be sure they were safe."

"What does this have to do with the Wyatts?" Sarah asked. Her voice was flat and emotionless, but her hand had come up to grip Dev's on her shoulder.

"Your mother had been involved with Ace Wyatt."

The hand that had been clutching his fell off and into her lap. She didn't say anything, so Duke continued. But Dev knew what those little gestures meant. She didn't want any kind of link with a Wyatt.

Even him.

Still, he couldn't bring himself to pull his hand off her shoulder and leave her sitting there absorbing all that information without some kind of understanding. Connections to monsters he knew all too well.

"Ace and your mother had a son before she managed to leave," Duke continued. "She met your father, started a new life. Or thought she had."

"Anth Wyatt is the son," Sarah said, her voice even flatter. She slid her hands over her belly, that protective gesture.

It wasn't about him, but it still made Dev feel like slime. He'd known Anth was out there and hadn't used that as a reason to keep her at arm's length when it came to the whole helping her have a baby thing.

"Yes. They knew Eva and I would take good care of their child, and they knew that being close to Pauline Reaves wouldn't hurt any."

Sarah swallowed loudly, though absolutely no emotion showed on her face. "My...parents. Are they..."

"They both died, sweetheart. I'm sorry." Duke sighed heavily. "Eva and I had agreed that if Ace wasn't a threat anymore, we'd tell you. Once he finally wasn't, it didn't seem any good to stir up a hornet's nest."

Sarah was quiet for a long time, and Dev and Duke stood in silence, letting her decide what to say next.

"But right now the threat is against you." She looked up at Dev. Her blue eyes weren't accusing, but Dev wasn't accustomed to the cold light in them.

"My brothers and I got notes, yes."

"I didn't get one. The threat wasn't against me. If everything you're saying is true, he doesn't even know—"

"We don't know what he knows, Sarah. Which means we need to take all the precautions we can." Dev tried to say what needed to be said gently, but his words came out harsh.

It shouldn't be so hard to protect someone. Sarah always made it far more difficult than it had to be. This pregnancy was no exception, and because he was already tired of worrying over her on that score, he was not going to tiptoe around this.

"We don't know what Anth is capable of. We don't know what ways Ace warped him. In the moment, I thought him helping me was charity or a conscience. Now…"

"Now what?"

"I think it was just like Ace. To let me think I'd survived. To think I was free and clear, only to have a note show up that things aren't over. I think it was a plan—whether between the two of them or Anth alone—so that when it would hurt even more, he could come after me."

He kneeled in front of Sarah, because she had to get it through her thick skull that protecting her was the only thing that mattered. "Maybe he doesn't know about you, Sarah, but it wouldn't take much digging for him to figure it out. We won't know when or if he does, and our baby is going to be here sooner rather than later. I know you'd do everything in your power to protect him, so let us do everything in our power to protect you."

Sarah opened her mouth, but whatever she was going to say was lost in Duke's booming voice.

In an instant Duke squared off with Dev and demanded, "You better explain that, because it sure as hell sounded like you just said *our* baby."

Chapter Five

Sarah's heart leaped into her throat. Dev had said *our* baby.

In front of Dad, yes, which was less than ideal. Less than less ideal, if she was being honest. But he'd… In the midst of all his awfulness he'd talked about protecting *our* baby. As if he held some ownership in this child. The way she'd desperately wanted him to.

She blinked at the silly tears and swallowed down the laugh that wanted to bubble over at the utter *horror* in Dev's eyes as Duke waited furiously for an explanation. Clearly Dev had not meant to say *our*, but that made it all the more special—it meant he felt it, even if he didn't want to admit it.

Though she was moved by the admission, hoped it was the starting point for Dev to see he had this little life to truly live for, she tried to smooth things over. "Dev just meant the royal *our*. You know. This baby is all of ours," Sarah said, her voice squeaky. It was with emotion, but she was a little afraid Duke would read it as nerves.

"Bull," Duke spat. "Explain this, Wyatt."

Sarah winced. Dad using a last name was *never* good. Dev slowly stood from his kneeling position at her chair. His expression was hard and that blank look that had her heart pinching in her chest.

She was desperate to get rid of that default reaction in him. She tried to scoot off the chair, but it was an ungainly struggle and she gave up on a huff as Dev and Duke stared at each other in a silent standoff. "Don't we have more important things to—"

"Are you the father?" Duke demanded, wholly unconcerned with *her* at the moment.

Which had her temper bubbling up over the giddy hope she'd been feeling. She managed to get to her feet this time and stepped in between Dev's motionless, emotionless form and Duke's furious one.

"Dad! I got pregnant because I wanted to have a baby."

Duke's gaze finally left Dev's and met hers. "With him?"

She met his fury with her own. "I wanted a baby, and I didn't want a baby daddy. So Dev did me a favor and supplied the…necessary components."

She heard Dev groan behind her and Duke winced a little bit at that himself. Well, good, if she could make both men uncomfortable, maybe they'd stop being angry or defensive or *whatever*.

"It was my choice and I begged him to do it. Trust me, he didn't want to. He did me a favor."

"I…can't pretend to understand any of this," Duke said, shaking his head.

"You don't need to. Anth Wyatt is threatening six of us." The mention of the real reason they were here sobered both men. "I'll move into Pauline's as long as you do too, Dad. I think it's good for as many of us as possible to be under the same roof. That way we can always pair up to do the chores. Someone can always be with me. It makes sense. You staying here alone does not make sense."

"You're changing the subject," Duke said, crossing his arms over his chest.

"For the time being. Because protecting ourselves is a little more important than you acting like you have a say in the matter—" she pointed at her large stomach "—when we're already here."

Duke's gaze moved back to Dev behind her. Narrowed and angry. Sarah didn't have to look at Dev to know what the expression on his face would be. Blank. Maybe with the ghost of self-loathing.

"I'd say both are pretty important," Duke said at length.

"I'd say it's not between you and Dev to work out. It's between you and me," Sarah argued. "And I'm not speaking another word about it until we're all together at Grandma Pauline's." With that, she turned on a heel and marched—or, more accurately, waddled—out of the room.

She had to use the banister for support to help get her up the stairs. She didn't feel any contractions but she felt *heavy* as she huffed and puffed up to her room.

"I'm mostly ready to get you out of there, little man, but you're probably safer inside and, oh yeah,

I'm terrified of pushing you out of me." She rubbed her stomach, comforted by the little conversation with her baby. Maybe he was just hearing garbled nonsense in there, but it was *her* garbled nonsense.

She wasn't afraid of being a mother. She'd watched Felicity and Gage deal with the demands of pregnancy and a newborn. Sarah knew it would be hard and exhausting, but she also knew she'd have help and love to get through it.

But no matter how she told herself she'd watched horses and cattle birth their young—and if they could do it out there with no intervention, she could certainly do it in a hospital with an epidural—the worry and fear of actual labor were overwhelming at times.

Now she didn't have to just fear labor, she had to fear Anth Wyatt. Not just Dev's half brother, but her own.

She couldn't wrap her head around it. Her mother had conceived a child with Ace Wyatt. This biological mother she'd never known—but Duke had.

She stood in her room trying to work out how she felt about it, but there were too many realities assaulting her to get too wrapped up in the past at the moment. She was so pregnant she didn't even want to sit down for fear of not wanting to get back up. The Wyatts were being threatened, which left her sisters all in a dangerous position. Duke knew Dev was the father of her baby and she'd left them downstairs to squabble pointlessly.

How could she stand here and try to understand

the mother and father she'd never known, who were dead anyway?

She had to focus on the task at hand, which was packing some things so she could spend the next few days at Grandma Pauline's with the rest of her family. Grandma Pauline's house was big, with all sorts of hodgepodge rooms added on over the years, but it'd still be a tight fit even if Jamison's and Cody's families stayed in Bonesteel.

She found a duffel bag and packed all of her over-size sweats that managed to fit over her pregnant belly. She tossed in her pregnancy book and set her body pillow next to the bag on the bed. If she forgot something, she could always come back and get it. The houses weren't that far apart, and just because they were in danger didn't mean the ranch work got to stop. They'd have to keep going back and forth for the time being.

She heard footsteps on the stairs down the hall. She knew it wasn't Duke. He didn't take the steps that fast or with that much…the word *menace* floated through her mind. But what was menacing about Dev? That he was grumpy? She'd handled that forever.

Or is the thing you can't handle the fact he said our baby like it matters?

Well.

When he appeared at her doorway, he stayed right there. "Duke's packing. You shouldn't be carrying anything you need, so I will when you're done."

He stood there looking grumpy, which was his norm, but there was a way he held himself—hands deep in his pockets, gaze refusing to meet hers—that told her he was also very uncomfortable. Not just because he'd never been in her bedroom before, but she was sure because he'd spilled the beans.

He'd said *our baby*.

She couldn't fight away the tide of emotion. The want she kept trying to convince herself she didn't have. Duke knew he was the father because... "You said *our* baby," she managed on a whisper.

"It doesn't matter." His voice was flat. So were his eyes.

She could be devastated by that, but she'd never been any good at letting other people dictate how she felt or what she should think. "It matters to me."

"This isn't a fairy tale, Sarah. You don't want it to be. Let's just—"

"Do you want it to be?"

Some of his composure cracked and he raked his hands through his dark hair. "No," he said emphatically, but there was something wild in his expression—far closer to fear than denial.

"So, it's not a fairy tale. That doesn't mean it can't be something... It doesn't mean you have to close yourself off from him. He's ours."

"Nothing is mine."

He just cracked her heart in two. She moved to him and touched his face, couldn't seem to *stop* touching him lately when she'd always been the perfect paragon of restraint. She wasn't a touchy-feely person and the random want to touch Dev was always shoved ruthlessly away.

But this baby, and this danger, it changed things... whether she'd planned on it or not. Then there was this old Dev she thought he'd moved past.

"Please don't go back there," she said.

"Back where?"

"To that awful shell you were after you came home from the hospital. I know this is hard, and I know you've got your guilt complex, and this weird idea you're somehow less than your brothers, but for ten years you have slowly stepped out of that and into the land of the living. It would break my heart if you lost all that."

He looked at her like she'd lanced him straight through—which didn't bother her because it was emotion, not blankness. And he *looked* at her—met her gaze and didn't turn away.

There was too much emotion swirling inside of her, too many of the feelings she usually convinced herself were silly fantasies. It was hard here in her room, touching him, her belly between them. Especially when he didn't move away from her hand, just stood there looking down at her.

And she wanted to kiss him. It wasn't all that unheard of a feeling. Throughout her teenage years she'd convinced herself she found him *repulsive*. And obnoxious. He was still obnoxious, but when she'd made any attempts to date outside the ranch, she compared every guy to Dev.

And they all were lacking. Still, even after she'd accepted that—that he was, for whatever reason, the only man she was ever going to truly be able to give her heart to—she'd been completely and utterly determined to just keep her heart to herself.

She didn't touch him. She didn't flirt with him. She *had* asked him for a baby, but she'd been determined to leave it at that.

For the first time in her life, something had blown up in her face. Even without remembering all of it, she knew he was it for her. And he was looking at her. She was touching him. Danger was encroaching.

Why not go for broke?

She rose to her toes and pressed her mouth to his. He didn't exactly kiss her back, but he didn't push her away or dart off. He let her move her mouth softly against his, igniting a memory of the night they'd conceived their child.

He'd told her not to kiss him and that they should just get it over with. So she'd kissed him right then and there in the hotel hallway because he did *not* get to tell her what to do—drunk or sober.

Except all those months ago he'd kissed her back, with a passion that had surprised her then and now as she remembered it. Could that have really been Dev? Kissing her? Was her memory just some overactive imagination…when she'd never had one of those before?

She couldn't hold herself up on her tiptoes any longer, so she had to pull away, back to her normal height.

DEV GENTLY PUSHED Sarah back a full step. Then he took his own steps backwards and away from *her*.

Why had she kissed him? Why had he let her? Everything was messed up and he could not let that continue.

"I'm sure that was pregnancy hormones or something," he muttered, offering her *any* excuse to let this go.

But fury leaped into her eyes and her hand balled into a fist. "No, this is pregnancy hormones or something." And before he realized what she was doing, she landed a jab right in his gut. He bent over with an *oof*, the air whooshing out of his lungs.

He straightened his shoulders, sucked in a breath and glared at her. "Pack your bag, Sarah."

"It's packed, *Devin*. I have to grab my toiletries." With that she sailed out of the room like some queen on high, belly and all.

Dev huffed. *Women*. He grabbed the duffel off the bed and slung it over his shoulder, stuffing the pillow under his arm. It *was* pregnancy hormones. And fear. Because Sarah had never been so gentle with him. She'd never given him stark honesty about the state he'd been in after his injuries…or the way he'd slowly crawled out of the dark space.

Not that he'd crawled into a *light* space. He wasn't an optimistic guy, and he *wasn't* as good as his brothers—that much was certain in a million different ways. He didn't want the families they were building, but he also wanted to, well, live. Take care of the ranch and Grandma. It had taken him a few years of being in a bad place to get there, but he had gotten there.

Would he go back? Just because a truth he'd hidden had come back to bite him in the butt? Would he fight off that feeling just because Sarah had said it would break her heart if he didn't?

He grumbled to himself all the way down the stairs. Duke was already ready, standing in the kitchen. When Dev entered, he glowered.

Dev sighed. "She's getting her toiletries."

Duke huffed. "Good. I have more to say to you. Whatever she thinks, I *do* have a say in all this. I'm her father and it's my job to protect her. I don't know what the hell you were thinking, but—"

He'd been thinking he could give Sarah something, no strings attached. He'd been thinking he could feel like some kind of help for once. Of course, he'd never actually felt any of those things, even before this moment, but *that's* what he'd been thinking.

"—you will do right by her."

Dev shook his head. He wasn't going to explain himself to Duke. Or anyone, for that matter. "Hate me if you want, Duke, but this is between..." Except it wasn't between anybody. It was up to him. He'd done what Sarah had asked of him, and now they had to keep it a secret at all costs. "I get to decide what's right, and it clearly isn't whatever you think is."

Duke's brow furrowed and he studied Dev with a sincerity and perception that made Dev shift uncomfortably on his feet.

"You *want* me to hate you," Duke said after a while, as if it was some dawning realization.

Dev snorted, perhaps a little too loud. He didn't want anyone to hate him. He just wanted everyone to understand things were better when he was on the periphery. Didn't this whole thing with Anth *prove* that? "I don't want you to—"

"You do. You want to feel guilty. You want everyone to hate you so you can mope around this ranch feeling sorry for yourself. So you can keep yourself separate and consider it noble. You might have gotten away with that for too long, but time's up. You've got people to protect, and a baby to be a father to—whether that's Sarah's plan or not."

Panic bloomed in his chest, but something bigger than that. Fear. A blinding, terrifying fear. At the word *father*. At Sarah depending on him to protect her, when he knew he wasn't any good at that. "It's not her plan." His voice was too rusty, but he couldn't let Duke think any of what he wanted was ever going to come to fruition. "She doesn't want a partner in this. She—"

"Bull. She wants *you* as a partner, boy. God knows why."

Dev thought of that kiss, but refused to accept what Duke was saying. Sarah was…churned up. Maybe she didn't want to call it hormones, but she wasn't herself. She'd have the kid and go back to being… Sarah. Real Sarah who didn't touch him or cut him open with a few words, showing just how well she saw through him. "I can't… Don't you see the danger that puts her in?"

"I've got five of my daughters married to or living with your brothers. I tried to warn every last one of them off, because trouble is in the Wyatt name and in the Wyatt blood. Boy, I know. I was like you once upon a time. But they all chose love and life over fear. You might not have that in you, Dev, but Sarah sure does."

With that, he took the duffel out of Dev's hands and headed for the door. Leaving Dev alone, holding a body pillow, with far too many revelations, and way worse, far too many emotions.

Chapter Six

Sarah woke up in a strange bed. For all the hubbub, and the giant stomach impeding any comfortable movement, she had slept pretty well. At least imminent danger couldn't disrupt her sleep schedule like a baby was inevitably going to.

She ran her hands over her stomach in her morning ritual. She whispered a few greeting words to the baby, tried out names like she did every morning, and then finally forced herself to get out of bed.

She'd help Grandma Pauline wash up after breakfast. Then maybe she could talk to Duke about her parents.

Her chest got too tight. Her parents were dead, and they'd given her away to protect her. For so long Sarah had done everything she could not to think about them, to convince herself she was better off without them and vice versa—she didn't want to know if they were good or bad people because both options were awful.

Now, both options were pointless because they were dead.

And her mother had been impregnated by Ace Wyatt. So she did have something in common with her mother, one way or another.

There was one big difference, of course. Dev wasn't Ace. He might be grumpy and have a guilt complex the size of the Badlands, but he was a good man. He watched over his grandmother, took care of the ranch—and helped with hers and Duke's when they were needing it. He was grumbly and contentious, but it hid a kindness he couldn't fight no matter how much he seemed to want to.

"You'll never have to wonder if your father is a good man," she promised her boy.

Except, how could she keep that promise if Dev was determined to be nothing more than sperm donor?

Our baby.

All this time she'd held onto a hope that *our* would mean something. Shouldn't she just keep holding on to that hope until this danger with Anth passed? What was more important: feelings or surviving a lunatic making threats against some of the most important people in her life?

She heaved herself out of bed. Too much thinking for one morning. Besides, a giant baby kicking her bladder wasn't exactly the stuff relaxation was made of. She waddled across the hall and took care of the morning unpleasantry, then waddled right back to the room and threw on a few layers.

Even with pregnancy hormones and overheating, it was dang cold this morning. Of course by the time she'd managed to pull on socks she was breathing heavily.

No, she wouldn't miss pregnancy in the practical sense. Once dressed more warmly, she headed for downstairs. She knew Grandma Pauline had given her the room that best suited her needs—close to the bathroom, sandwiched between Grandma Pauline and the room Felicity and Gage were staying in so she had quick access to help if she needed any, but boy were the stairs something she dreaded.

Still, she could hardly kick Dev out of his room downstairs when he had an actual physical injury— one that pained him, especially in the winter and especially since he'd been doing extra ranch duty for months now.

It was very hard to be appreciative when she'd always prided herself on being so self-sufficient. She often had to remind herself it was for the baby, not her, before she snapped at some well-meaning family member or Wyatt brother.

As if thinking of one conjured one up, as she gripped the railing to help her down the stairs, Dev appeared below.

His nose was red with cold, and she had no doubt his leg was paining him, but more than that he looked tired, exhausted really. Dark shadows under his eyes, and slumped shoulders she'd learned meant he hadn't had a good night's sleep. "Looks like you had a rough night."

Dev grunted. "You look like a snowman."

She scowled at him. "It's cold. And I'm *pregnant*."

His mouth twitched a little, bordering on a smile. She wanted to really make him smile. Or laugh. Before the whole baby thing she'd been on a personal mission to get him to do both more, but then Brady and Cecilia's wedding plans and Rachel moving in with Tucker had made her feel a melancholy that could only be filled with achieving the next goal.

Motherhood.

Now she was here and it felt less like a goal to accomplish. She wasn't sure what it felt like instead, but nothing so cut and dried as a goal or an achievement. It was too big for that. Too all encompassing. Oddly like the danger they were in. She didn't know what lay ahead, or how to plan it out so things would go the way she wanted.

To an extent she was used to that with ranch life. Weather turned, cows died, years were bad. But the ranch and the land remained. People didn't necessarily.

"Grandma wanted me to come check on you. Having some problems with the heater."

Sarah forced herself to smile, still gripping the railing tightly. "I'll survive. I have all this extra insulation now."

He nodded, but he didn't move out of the stairway. He stared at her as if puzzling out some unsolved mystery.

Since she was familiar with that look, and that Dev might stand there and puzzle for a good few minutes before he got around to telling her what it was all about, she waited. She'd learned to have patience with Dev. Not that he'd ever see it that way. She still moved too fast and too decisively for him.

They balanced each other out rather nicely all in all.

"You kissed me," he finally said, eyebrows drawn together and voice equal parts lecturing and confused.

She crossed her arms over her chest, which meant resting them on her belly. "Yeah. So?"

Dev's gaze drifted there for a second and then back up to her face. "Duke's acting like…like you want more from me."

She wanted to curse her father, but instead she focused on the irritating man in front of her. "More than what?"

He scowled. "You know damn well what."

She didn't know why it hurt her feelings that he'd ask that. He had every right to speculate over her reasons for wanting him to be the father of her child. Which meant she'd have to give him a truth she wasn't too keen on laying at anyone's feet.

"I didn't get pregnant to trap you into having feelings for me if that's what you're asking. At the time, I wasn't too keen on having a Wyatt brother stomp my heart to bits, even if I did want his sperm."

Dev winced at the word *sperm* as she'd hoped he might. Honestly, men were so overly squeamish about some things. But his expression quickly sobered.

"What does 'at the time' mean?"

Sarah sighed. How could she explain how things had changed? How *she* had changed. How she wanted something from him, but didn't expect something from him. Hoped maybe, but not *expected*.

In the end, like so many things lately, it all boiled down to their baby. She unfolded her arms and placed her palms on either side of the round lump. "I love this baby and I don't even know him yet. I can't imagine what it'll feel like when he's real and in my arms and I'm in charge of keeping him alive. I've had to come to terms with being that vulnerable, and I imagine I've got a ways to go, but I'm not so afraid of it anymore."

"Of what?"

"Love."

Any confusion or effort to understand disappeared from his face. Emotion shuttered away to blankness. It made her want to cry, but she blinked back the tears.

For a moment, he'd wanted to know. Maybe he didn't like her answers, but he'd wanted to understand.

"Grandma will be wanting to feed you now that you're up," he grumbled, then turned on a heel and disappeared down the stairs.

Sarah stayed where she was for a few moments. It was hard to let him walk away, because she was better suited to be a bulldozer. Still, she'd learned a thing or two. Dev needed a good hard push sometimes, but more often than not he needed time to work out a problem to his own satisfaction. He was an internal kind of guy.

It was just a shame so often he came to the *wrong* conclusion, that she'd have to talk him out of.

DEV FELT AS IF someone had shoved a cattle prod into his chest. There was a disquieting, painful buzzing lodged there and no matter how much distance he put between him and Sarah, it remained.

What the hell was she talking about *love* for?

He paused outside the kitchen. Too many of his family members were in there and would read something in his expression, in his demeanor. He needed a moment to bury it.

He took a deep breath and listened to the voices in the kitchen.

"I think town is the safer option when she's *that* pregnant."

Dev closed his eyes. Oh, they couldn't be so stupid as to think they could make a decision about Sarah without her in the room. She would not handle that well *at all*.

He glanced back at the stairs. She'd waited to follow him, but not long. She took the last step and moved toward him, her expression oddly…blank.

He wasn't sure he'd ever seen that kind of expression on her face before. She was a woman who was not afraid to show how she felt. Well, that wasn't true. She didn't care to show off sad or sweet, but pregnancy had brought down some of those walls.

God help him.

She came to stand next to him and cocked her head.

"We need to convince her it's her own idea. She'll

never agree if we tell her to do it. We'll have to be careful about how we approach her..."

Dev closed his yes. Oh, no. No, no, no. This was not going to go well. When he reopened them and glanced down at Sarah he saw just what he'd expected.

Wild, untethered fury.

"Sarah, why don't you calm down before—"

She shook her head and brought her fingers to her lips.

"I'm not going to stand here and eavesdrop," he whispered to her, though he supposed the whispering kind of undercut his grand stand against listening in.

"We'll just pretend it's random," Cecilia was saying from inside the kitchen. "Sarah, Dev, and Rach and Tucker. That's four in town. Four in Bonesteel, and leaves us five here. It's not such a bad split."

Dev felt his own anger begin to simmer. That wasn't just *random*. He and Rachel both had physical limitations, what with Rachel being legally blind. It wasn't just *coincidence* they thought it was a good idea to ship him into town.

When he had a ranch to run *and* was the whole reason danger was at their doorstep in the first place.

Sarah raised an eyebrow at him and gave him a smirk, as if to say *see, I'm not overreacting.*

Dev grunted and charged in, though Sarah was right at his heels. The conversation came to a clear stop as they entered. Felicity and Cecilia were standing in the kitchen area, likely helping Grandma Pauline with kitchen duties. Gage was sitting at the table, helping feed his daughter breakfast.

Dev knew Brady, Tucker, Duke and Rachel were out doing chores at both ranches, but would likely be in soon. He hoped they would be here soon enough to get an earful.

"So, you have to be careful huh?" Sarah demanded of her sisters, hands on her hips.

Felicity and Cecilia shared a look, while Grandma Pauline kept cleaning and Gage kept feeding.

Felicity sighed. "Now, Sarah. We're only trying to look out for you. You should be close to the hospital. That's just common sense," Felicity insisted.

"How come up to this point it was common sense to keep us all together?"

"We're not saying you should stay in town alone, Sarah," Cecilia replied.

"No, you want to ship the guy with the limp off with her," Dev added. "Like some sort of weakest link eradication."

Cecilia frowned at him. "You're both being overly sensitive. We're working out best options to keep *everyone* safe, including and most especially the children." She gestured at Sarah's stomach.

"Why on earth would she be safe with me? I think we're well aware I'm a big part of the target here. I got a note just like the rest of my brothers. I'm the one who actually *knows* Anth. Why don't you women take her off to town? No one's threatening you."

"Oh, Dev," Gage said sadly.

Dev didn't even have time to ask Gage what he

meant before all four women in the kitchen were glaring daggers at him. Even one-year-old Claire seemed to give him a dirty look.

The door to the mudroom opened and Tucker and Brady came in, though they both stopped short at the tension in the room.

"Abort. Save yourselves," Gage muttered, earning him a light slap on the shoulder from his wife before Felicity swooped in and picked up Claire.

"I'll just go change her and you all can have the knock-out drag-out fight you're so desperate to have." She stopped in front of Sarah, expression going sad. "I hope you know we're all just looking out for you."

If Sarah was mollified, she didn't show it. She turned her anger toward Brady and Tucker at the door. "So, which scenario do you two agree with?"

"Uh," Tucker said. "What were the options again?"

"What happens if you're stuck out here in labor while there's danger?" Cecilia demanded of Sarah, ignoring Tucker's question.

"What happens if I'm off in town in labor while there's danger? Not much different, to my way of thinking."

"A lot quicker to get you to the hospital though. Brady agrees with me," Cecilia said resolutely. "Everyone agrees because it's the most sensible, reasonable option."

Sarah took exception to that. Brady tried to smooth things over, which only got *his* wife angry at him. Gage cracked a joke which made *everyone* mad until the voices all rose over each other and the entire kitchen was just an unholy din that made Dev's temples pound.

The clanging bell echoed through the kitchen, making everyone wince, but also bringing the arguing and shouting to a dead silence. No one dared break it until Grandma Pauline said her piece.

"How did we weather last year?" she demanded. "Going off in different directions? A few of you did, and what happened? I'll tell you what happened. You got your butts kicked—every time—except when you got it through your thick skulls to ask for help. Now you." Grandma Pauline turned and pointed at Sarah.

Sarah blinked, even kind of leaned toward Dev as if she could hide behind him and avoid Grandma's lecture.

"You're nine months pregnant in the dead of winter and acting like a stubborn mule. And you!" She moved the pointed finger to him. "Are acting like an egotistical teenager who can't get it through his head that not *everything* is about him." She huffed out a breath. "And the rest of you are shouting out orders without asking anyone how they feel about them—which is not how a family does things. Now, we're going to start over, and we're going to act like a family—*not* a military institution, *not* a high school cafeteria, and most especially *not* like one of those god-awful reality TV programs."

"That you love to watch," Gage muttered, ever attempting to lighten a moment.

Sarah sighed heavily, massaging her stomach like

she did when it was paining her but not a contraction. "Grandma's right. We need to talk. Really talk. And I think most of all, we need to stick together." She looked up at Dev, something unreadable in her expression. "How can one man beat us if we all stick together?"

Dev didn't know how to answer that question. The truth was, Ace had always seemed to win—even escaping the Sons of the Badlands, even being raised by Grandma Pauline, it hadn't saved them from everything. Not the first terrible years of their childhood. Not their mother's death. It certainly hadn't solved any of the rage inside of him that he'd forever be cursed by who and what his father was.

Even now, Ace was dead, but they were still in danger. Still trying to figure out how to fight bad with good—almost as if good could never permanently win.

But Sarah rubbed her stomach and something shifted in his chest. There was a baby in there—one that would be making his appearance very soon. That baby didn't deserve to be born into a world of fear and gravity. He didn't deserve what Dev had been forced to endure as a child.

Maybe Dev had a hard time believing good could win—maybe he'd even given up on truly winning— but there was a child that needed more from him than giving up.

"He won't beat us," Dev managed. Maybe he'd failed everything up to this point, and maybe he'd never be a father to that child, but the baby *was* his. Part of him. Part of Sarah.

No matter the consequences, he'd fight to give that baby something better.

Chapter Seven

Trying to find consensus amidst the varying opinions of fourteen people was, to Sarah's way of thinking, impossible.

She'd managed to talk almost everyone out of the whole ship-her-off-to-town plan—at least for another few days. Everyone wanted to "reevaluate" after her doctor's appointment on Tuesday.

Eventually she'd given up. She'd tried to help Grandma Pauline with kitchen chores but had been shooed away. She'd tried to help Felicity with Claire, but Claire had been taking a nap and, well, it sounded like a fine idea to Sarah.

She was tired and uncomfortable and grumpy, and a good sleep in a quiet room was just what she needed. Especially since no one would let her *do* anything.

But it would require the endless trek up the stairs. Sarah looked up the staircase. Never in her life had it looked so gigantic. May as well have been Mount Everest.

She could go doze on the recliner in the living room, but with so many people coming and going it wouldn't be very restful. It also wasn't the image she wanted to present right now. She didn't want people to see her tired or worn out—they'd worry about the drive time to the hospital and anything else.

No, better to do the resting in her own room.

Still, she stood at the bottom of the stairs, grimacing, and wishing there was any other option.

She heard footsteps behind her, turned to see Dev step into the hallway. He still had his coat on, though it was unzipped, plus a stocking hat and gloves.

"You okay?"

Sarah let out a hefty sigh. "I want to take a nap. My bed is very far away."

He seemed to consider this, then started walking toward her. "Come on," he grumbled. He made a move like he was going to take her arm, but in the end he just kept walking, passed her and then went into the short hallway that led to his room.

Growing up it had been a laundry room, but after Dev's accident he hadn't been able to use the stairs for quite some time so his brothers had renovated the room into a bedroom.

She imagined he could move upstairs now, but he hadn't.

He pointed at his bed—which was made. An odd detail to notice, but she never made her bed. Then again Duke hadn't been a stickler for household cleanliness like Grandma Pauline was.

"Knock yourself out."

"You're going to let me sleep in your bed?"

"Yeah. Why not?"

An excellent question. It wasn't a big deal or anything all that amazing—but the idea of crawling into his bed had her thinking about an intimacy she didn't have with him.

You've slept together.

But not in one of their beds. Not even in one of their houses. It had been in a hotel room and she barely remembered it.

He won't be in bed with you now. Get a grip.

Right. "Well, what are you going to do?"

He pulled a drawer open and grabbed a pair of thick socks. "Told Tuck I'd let him borrow a pair since he's a moron who stepped in a giant puddle. Just getting these to take back out to him. Lots of chores to do."

So he was doing chores with Tuck. Which was good. No one was going off on their own.

And it was weird standing in his room with him. "Well, thanks for the bed."

He shrugged. "No problem. Door doesn't lock but I'll let everyone know so they don't bother you."

"Oh, don't do that. I don't want them thinking I need a nap."

"But you do need a nap."

"I don't *need* one. I want one because nobody will let me do anything. But if they're worried I'm too tired or whatever it starts the move-me-to-town discussion all over again."

"It isn't such a terrible idea."

She frowned up at him. "See?"

"It's a good thirty miles to the hospital from here. If the roads are bad when you're in labor…"

"I've discussed that with my doctor, Dev. She wasn't concerned. First-time labor is rarely fast, and so far my contractions are sporadic at worst."

"Well, we'll see what she says next week, won't we?" His expression changed as she massaged her side. She wasn't feeling any contractions, just a general ache of her stomach being stretched to capacity.

His expression now was like the expression he'd gotten on his face when he'd started saying Anth wouldn't beat them. A determination and fire she couldn't remember seeing in him since he'd been a teenager. It made her heart do wild windmills in her chest.

"I could come with," he said after a long while.

"To my doctor's appointment?"

"Yeah."

The cartwheeling died because it was no kind offer. It wasn't about wanting to be a part of it. "You just want to make sure I don't lie about what the doctor says."

He held her gaze, so serious and…direct. "No."

"Then why?" Sarah demanded. She wasn't falling for it. She knew him well enough to know this was all about having his way. Not about…what she wanted it to be about.

"Listen. If we settle things with Anth—"

"When we beat him, you mean."

"Sure, whatever. I'm just saying, if there's no danger and everything is settled—"

"Everything will be settled. No *ifs* about it."

Dev scrubbed his hands over his face. "Why do you have to be so infuriating?"

"It's only infuriating because I'm right. Maybe you should just defer to me more often."

He snorted. "Like you'd want that. You live for an argument."

"I wouldn't go that far."

"I would."

"Seems to me that you're the one arg—"

"Would you shut up and let me say my piece before I change my mind?"

Sarah was surprised into silence if only because for as often as Dev got annoyed with her, argued and bickered with her, he rarely ever snapped in this way. A loss of temper. As if he was actually letting himself *care*.

"All right," she said, some odd mixture of anxiety and hope twining around her heart like a vise.

"You weren't totally off base about the guilt complex things and the less-than-my-brothers thing. I know I'm not as good as my brothers. I figure that's just fact, and you can close your big mouth and not argue with me for once so I can finish what I'm trying to say."

She snapped her mouth shut, though it took some willpower not to defend him to himself. Still, he was addressing a thing she'd said—a real, emotional, important thing. And that was some kind of amazing progress.

"But I'm not my father. I don't want to hurt anyone, and… Grandma was right. I've been thinking about my role in this whole thing selfishly. Who I am and what I am, but what Cecilia said about…protecting the children. The kid is part of me, even if I don't take any role as father. Maybe I'm not as noble or righteous as my brothers, but I… I had a bad father. The worst kind. I know what that's like, and I know how terrible the world can be, and no child deserves that."

"Our son would never…" She stopped herself from finishing the sentence when he glared at her.

He was trying to say…something. She might not understand where he was going, but it was important. He was actually showing her some of his feelings and emotions and she wanted to encourage that. Always.

"As long as Anth is dealt with, I want…" He blew out a long, tortuous breath. "I want to be part of it. Not passively like I was planning. But a father. A real father. The kind who protects his kid and gives him or her the best life he can."

Sarah couldn't remember a time she'd ever been fully speechless, but she couldn't think of a word to say. Not one word. All she could do was stand there, tears welling in her eyes and emotion clogging her throat.

His scowl deepened. "You said I could. You said you wanted me to."

Sarah nodded, trying to control her emotions that wanted to overflow. "I mean it," she managed to croak.

He shoved his hands into his pockets and scowled. "Well, good then. Anth has to be taken care of first, but… Once he is… Well. Yeah."

Sarah forced herself to take a deep breath. He wanted to be a father to their baby. It was what she'd hoped for, what she'd been certain *eventually* she'd be able to convince him to want as well. But this wasn't… As much as she'd believed he would, she hadn't ever considered how he'd tell her, or when, or what she'd want to say in response.

She should thank him. Or hug him. Or say it was good and take her nap, but Sarah had never been any good at not trying for the mile when an inch was given. "And what about us?"

Dev blinked then, looking a bit like he'd been stricken. "What do you mean?"

She knew full well he understood what she meant, but if he needed to hear it, so be it. "If you're going to be a dad, what does that make us?"

He took a step away from her, hands so deep in his pockets it was a wonder they didn't break through the fabric. "W-what we've always been. Friends."

"I don't think—"

Jamison appeared in the doorway, which had the words drying up in her mouth. Jamison was supposed to be in Bonesteel. Not standing in Dev's bedroom doorway, grave and imposing.

"Dev. Sarah. Sorry to interrupt, but we need you in the kitchen."

DEV WAS GLAD for the interruption, or so he thought until he walked into the kitchen and all his brothers were there and worse, so much worse, Liza—tear-stained and not doing anything to cover that up.

Liza who never cried. Who was so strong and tough and thumbed her nose at danger and threats.

"What is it?" Sarah asked.

Jamison sighed and gestured to the table. "This was nailed to my door this morning. At home."

Dev leaned forward with Sarah. A piece of paper lay on the table. It wasn't like the handwritten It's Not Over note. This had been typed and had a lot more text.

"It looks like a court document," Dev muttered.

"Not exactly."

Dev skimmed the writing on the paper, then went back to the beginning and read it word for word, his body getting colder and heart getting heavier.

Jamison Wyatt
Crimes:
    The subject has been the perpetrator of a wide variety of crimes since childhood. A history of lying, stealing, and the repeated, malicious torture and killing of his own kin.
Sentencing:
    For these acts of violence, treason and destruction, I do hereby sentence Jamison Wyatt to death. This will be meted out at the judge's discretion through the method J. Wyatt deemed acceptable through his own actions against his own brethren, for personal gain.
—AW

"I don't understand," Sarah whispered. "I don't understand."

"Kin and brethren. He means the Sons." Dev shook his head because he didn't understand either. "We didn't know he existed. How could Anth have anything to do with the Sons?"

"He was there, though, when Ace tried to kill you," Brady pointed out. "So at some point after we were out of the fold, he was brought in."

"I was in the fold," Liza said, her voice scratchy. "There were only a few years between when Jamison and I escaped and I went back to try and save my sister. He was never mentioned. I never once heard about some secret son of Ace's. I know they didn't trust me or anything, but I'm pretty sure I would have known about that."

"I take it no one else got one of these," Jamison said flatly.

Dev exchanged looks with his brothers. They all were just as bewildered as he was.

"It says one of six," Sarah said, her voice still little more than a whisper.

"What?" Jamison demanded.

Sarah leaned forward and pointed at the right-hand corner of the paper. In smaller text, there was a 1/6.

"I just figured it was the number of pages printed out," Liza said, frowning down at the paper.

"Six is no coincidence. He's not singling you out," Dev muttered. "He's taking us one by one."

Liza buried her face in her hands. "This is supposed to be over."

She was right. It was supposed to be over. For all of them. He should have told this secret last year—if he had, maybe it would be over.

But he couldn't rewind and fix things then—so he

had to fix them now. He looked back at the paper. "Look. He's given us this document. It's some kind of warning. He could have just taken us all out, one by one, last year. He's had all this time. Instead he's doing some elaborate Ace-like plan. Which means we've got the time to shore up our protections. Maybe there are even clues in this thing. Maybe it gives us the opportunity to work through it before he can do anything."

"And if we can't?" Liza demanded. She glared up at Dev, but tears were tracking down her cheeks.

"Liza…" Jamison said, sounding wounded.

"We stick together," Brady said firmly. "We protect each other. It got us through last year. It'll get us through this."

"If there are clues here, and we can figure them out, we can be ready for him. Not just keep Jamison safe, but take Anth down. He's giving us the opportunity to win. He's giving us a fair fight."

"None of this is fair," Liza said, pushing away from the table. "I need some air," she muttered, then slammed out of the kitchen.

Jamison closed his eyes, then rubbed his hands over his face. Sarah gave him a pat on the shoulder.

"I'll go sit with her."

He nodded grimly. Once both women were gone, Jamison slowly turned back to them. For a few seconds, all six of them stood in the kitchen in utter silence.

Dev had promised himself he'd fight for his child, but now his brother had been specifically singled out. He didn't need any realizations to know what to do now.

"It's one of six. Which means we have six chances—six chances not just to fight Anth, but to take him down. He's taking us one by one. And warning us. There's something to this…performance. Some code or something—like Ace had."

"Good. Another Ace to fight," Brady said disgustedly.

"Who knows if he's the only one?" Tucker added.

"He's the only one," Dev replied. "There's no way Ace could have kept multiple children a secret. He certainly wouldn't have time to warp all of them."

"You hope," Brady said.

"This is it. I'm sure of it. Our last ghost to fight."

"How can you be sure of it?" Jamison asked, his gaze still on the door Liza had gone out of.

"Nothing else adds up," Dev said. "Maybe Ace was crazy. Maybe the Sons are evil. But the numbers always add up. Anth is our last hurdle. The North Star group has mostly disbanded the Sons. All those federal raids left them with next to no resources, loyalty or power. If there was anyone else to come after us, Anth would have recruited them. We would have heard Sons rumblings. But no, they've been thrown in jail or they ran. All that's left is Anth, and us. So we just have to figure out what he's trying to tell us and beat him at his own game."

"If we can stay alive," Jamison muttered.

"The Sons haven't beaten us yet, Jamison. I don't intend for that to change, do you?" Dev demanded.

Gage chuckled. "He sounded just like you, J." Gage gave a mock shiver. "Downright creepy."

Jamison frowned at Gage, but his expression had changed. The hurt and worry over Liza were still there, but that battle light was back. He looked down at the paper. "What kind of clues could there be?"

"Let's read it again—line by line—and go from there." Dev took an empty seat and waited for Jamison to take the other one. He looked at each of his brothers, sitting around Grandma Pauline's table. They'd been here before—too many times to count.

This would be the last time. Dev was determined. "We'll beat him. We have to." There were too many lives at stake not to.

Chapter Eight

Sarah wasn't sure she'd ever seen Liza so visibly distraught, and Liza had not had an easy life. She'd been in danger for most of it. So it was beyond concerning she'd been so visibly upset—even if she had every right to be.

She was sitting on the back step. Cash sitting in front of her, wagging his tail as if waiting for a game of fetch. It was only then Sarah realized there was a mangy ball at Liza's feet.

Sarah moved to sit next to Liza on the back porch step, but it was a narrow step and would have been a tight fit even if she didn't have a giant belly impeding her way.

"For heaven's sake, don't sit here," Liza said, wiping her face with her sleeve. She popped to her feet. "You don't need to cheer me up."

"I'm not here to cheer you up. I'm just here to hold your hand. Also to throw that poor dog a ball since you won't."

Liza rolled her eyes, but she bent down and picked

up the ball. She heaved it with impressive power, and Cash took off like a bullet.

She turned to face Sarah, eyes puffy and face blotchy.

Sarah's heart twisted. She'd never seen Liza like this. "This isn't like you, Liza. You're usually more angry than…"

"A whiny, crying mess?"

"Well, I wasn't going to use those words."

Liza smirked, but it died quickly. She looked out over the horizon. It was cold, but there wasn't much of a wind today, so it was bearable in her heavy sweaters. Especially standing here in the midday sun.

Cash brought back the ball and Liza hurled it again.

"We really thought it was over, you know? That's the part I just can't… Our fathers are dead. The Sons are rubble. I shouldn't still have to be afraid."

"Does the fear ever really go away? Jamison is a sheriff's deputy. We both know that an illness can come in and take someone away. I think fear is just a part of loving."

Liza seemed to mull that over, but then she shook her head. "I don't think normal people have to fear the way we do."

"Maybe not, but I can't… We survived last year. Threat after threat and we worked together and survived and kept everyone safe. We weren't unscathed, but we're all together. I can't believe we won't be able to do that again."

Liza sighed heavily. "It's not that I don't think we

can survive. It's not even the fear exactly. I..." She kicked at the short railing. "We'd started the whole process to adopt."

"Oh, Liza."

"But we can hardly bring kids home with death threats nailed to the door." She shook her head, staring hard at the horizon. Cash hadn't reappeared with the ball. He'd bark occasionally, so Sarah assumed he was off chasing a squirrel or maybe Duke or Rachel coming in from the fields.

"We'd be really good parents to more than just Gigi. It isn't fair we can't give some kids what Duke and Eva gave us." Sarah was the only child Duke and Eva had adopted, but they'd fostered Sarah's four other sisters, and then had Rachel biologically. And Liza was right, they'd always given the girls—biological, adopted or fostered, a loving home. Even after Eva had died.

Sarah placed her hands on her own belly. So much of why she wanted to be a mother was because of Duke and Eva. She'd wanted to be like them—give like them, love like them.

Briefly she thought of Dev saying he actually wanted to be a father, and how much that gave Sarah the hope she could *really* be like Duke and Eva—a partnership raising kids together.

But Jamison being specifically targeted was a much bigger issue at hand. "We're going to survive this. All of us intact. When we do, you'll have your chance to adopt. I know it's an awful thing to have to put it off, but—"

"But what if this is the time we don't win, Sarah? Even if we do, how many times are we going to think it's over when it's not?" Liza's eyes were getting shiny again.

Cash's barking was growing incessant, but Sarah focused on Liza. "As many times as it takes, because… Well, you love Jamison. You always have."

"Of course I do."

"So, you can be mad at the circumstance. You can think it's unfair, because it is, but it's Jamison. So we'll all suck it up and keep him safe, whether we should have to or not. You can be mad as hell about that, Liza. No one's stopping you."

"You're trying to stop me with all this wisdom."

"It's not wisdom. It's just common sense. You can feel what you feel and still suck it up and do what you have to."

"Sarah sense. Life's a crapshoot so suck it up and do what you can."

Sarah lifted her hands. "Hard to argue with that kind of sense, isn't it?"

Liza stepped forward and pulled Sarah into a hug—which was notable since neither of them were particularly touchy-feely. Still, Sarah could tell Liza needed some kind of comfort. Jamison would comfort her too, but Liza would convince herself it was only to make her feel better—not because he actually believed that they could beat the threats against him.

"I do think they're right. The letter is a warning," Sarah said, hoping to soothe Liza more. "For whatever reason, this Anth wants us to know he's coming. Which gives us a much better chance to win."

"A man who can wait like this one has isn't stupid. If he's giving us a warning…" Liza shook her head. "That could be just to mess with our heads. After all, he accuses Jamison of killing his own kin and we know he hasn't and never would. I was with him all those years in the Sons, so I know. He didn't kill anyone."

"He's been responsible for the death of Sons members since leaving, though," Sarah pointed out, pulling away from Liza's arms. "Jailed some too, which may have led to their deaths, including Ace. If we look at it from their perspective, maybe Anth really does believe Jamison is responsible for killing his brethren. Maybe Ace made sure he believed it."

Liza grimaced. "I don't know how any of them could think the Sons were ever Jamison's kin, even when he was stuck in there. Even Ace."

"But you said it yourself. Another son of Ace's was never mentioned. No one named Anth was around when you were stuck in there. Maybe this guy only knows what Ace has told him about the Sons and the Wyatt brothers."

"Maybe. The horrible part is it's all possible. We at least *knew* Ace was our enemy before. Even knowing he was a dangerous psychopath gave us something to go on. We don't know anything about Anth Wyatt."

Sarah thought about the fact that she did. She knew that she shared blood with the man. That her mother had been afraid enough of her own son to ask someone else to take her brand-new baby with another man.

Technically, she herself was Anth's kin and brethren too. Did he know that? Did he consider the Wyatt brothers his kin? And why had he used those two words? Repeatedly?

Cash's barking had stopped, but he hadn't run back with the ball. A little flutter of panic started in her chest, but Sarah pushed it away. There were a million things Cash could be out there chasing.

Including bad men.

Sarah whistled for him, called his name, but he didn't reappear.

Dread skittered up her spine. Wouldn't Anth expect Jamison to come right here after that letter—to his *real* brethren? Wouldn't he be able to plan some kind of ambush?

Sarah grabbed Liza's arm. "We have to get inside."

Liza's eyes widened, but she didn't argue. Clearly she understood Sarah's train of thought. She reached for the storm door, pulling it open. An explosion sounded and the glass shattered as they hurried through it. Sarah dropped to her knees. She tried to wriggle away from Liza, who was using her body to shield Sarah from the falling glass.

"You're going to get hurt," Sarah said, giving another ineffective push on Liza's body.

"That's the point. Better me than you and your baby. Can you crawl forward? Get to the main door?"

There was another gunshot, but no shattering glass this time.

"That came from inside," Liza said, pushing Sarah toward the door that led into the kitchen. "They're shooting back."

Sarah crawled over the concrete floor of the mudroom. It was awkward and painful in her current state, and the panicking beat of her heart didn't exactly help her arms stay steady as she tried to crawl without cutting herself on the glass.

She reached up to grab the knob, but another shot rang out, splintering into the house somewhere too close to Sarah for comfort. She snatched her hand back and huddled lower.

Liza scooted up next to her, but before she could pound on the door, it opened. Then, before Sarah had a chance to crawl forward, she was being pulled inside and immediately out of the doorway.

Despite her extra girth, Dev had moved her quite easily, Liza scurrying in behind her. Dev practically had Sarah in his lap by the time she looked around the room. Liza was sitting on the floor and leaning against the wall, breathing heavily. Jamison and Tucker were at the window above the kitchen sink, guns pointed out the opening. With no words spoken, Gage took the gun from Jamison and replaced him at the window. Jamison fell to his knees next to Liza.

"I'm okay," she said before Jamison could say or do anything. She reached out and cupped his cheek. "Might have a few cuts from the glass, but nothing serious. Would have been worse, but Sarah figured things out."

"I'm not sure I figured them out so much as Cash…

He was barking. Then he stopped." Sarah tried not to think the worst. After all, no gunshot had gone off before Cash's barking stopped. He couldn't have been killed. *Please*. Sarah looked up at Dev, who was smoothing down her hair. "He's out there."

"That's okay. He's a smart dog. He'll be all right," Dev said roughly.

Then another, more horrifying thought pierced Sarah's mind. She whipped her head toward Liza. "Is Gigi with Nina and Brianna?"

"And Cody. We told them about the note before coming here, so they're being careful," Liza said, but she had paled, and she looked to Jamison as if seeking reassurance.

No one mentioned that someone had snuck past all the security defenses Cody had set up around the property—and if someone could do that here, surely they could do it at Cody's house in Bonesteel.

"He didn't kill anyone, and he could have," Dev said. "Maybe this is just another warning."

But it was a warning with bullets, and Sarah knew that meant things were escalating. Danger was well and truly here, and they somehow had to find the strength to fight it again.

Whoever was out there stopped returning fire after Sarah and Liza were safely inside.

After minutes of endless waiting, there'd been a heated argument about how they would go about determining if the gunman had left, had been injured in return fire or was waiting them out.

Tucker had called Duke and Rachel immediately, having them take shelter at the Knight house since that's where they'd been closest to while dealing with the cattle feeding. He'd kept them on speakerphone, so if anything changed on their end, they'd know about it right away and could send help. Brady had Cody on speakerphone for the same reason.

Grandma Pauline was upstairs with Felicity and Claire, and Cecilia was still at work at the reservation. They'd texted her to stay put for the time being.

"It's been long enough. If we don't go out soon, we're going to lose daylight," Jamison said, pacing the length of the kitchen.

"Maybe that's what he's counting on," Liza insisted.

"Maybe, but how will we know if some of us don't look?" Dev asked. He was doing his best to remain still, to remain calm. Not to let his brain go back to when that gunshot had gone off and they hadn't known if Liza and Sarah were okay.

It had been a brief second before Tucker had looked out the window and been able to see them crawl inside. But it had been a terrible, bleak second.

"Any luck on those cameras, Cody?" Brady said into his phone.

"No. Whatever he did, he cut my mainframe. I don't have any video feed—or anything recorded."

"How would he do that?" Dev asked.

"Not a clue." Cody didn't have to be in the same physical space as Dev for him to be able to read Cody's frustration.

"We have to do a sweep," Jamison demanded. "Nobody goes alone, and we don't do anything stupid. But we have to look."

"He's right," Gage added. "We can't just sit in here and twiddle our thumbs. Especially when we know he's cut the video. Who knows what other security measures Cody put up have been tampered with?"

"Why don't two of you search the main area around the house. Have Duke and Rachel drive over, keeping an eye out on that end. I'll pack up the girls here and drive for you guys—which will give me a look around the highway side of the property. There's no way we can reach everything, but we can scope out a lot."

"He's right," Dev agreed. "If we do a quick sweep and don't find anything, we'll need all hands on deck to keep a lookout through the night."

Liza scowled, but she didn't pose an argument.

"Rachel and I are on our way," Duke said from Tucker's speakerphone.

"Nina and I will be on our way with the girls in a few," Cody said from Brady's speakerphone.

"We'll go out," Dev said to Jamison. "Search around the house and the stables."

"Why you?" Sarah demanded at the same time Liza did.

"I know where everything should be better than anyone," Dev said to Sarah. "And Jamison is the best shot," he said to Liza.

"Well, now, I wouldn't go *that* far," Gage muttered.

"He is and we all know it. So, he'll have my back and I can see if anything is off."

"Don't you think we should all agree and not just listen to orders from you?" Sarah said. She looked terribly uncomfortable, fidgeting in the kitchen chair like she couldn't find a position that didn't hurt her back. They'd tried to convince her to lie down or at least go relax in the recliner in the living room, but she'd refused.

"We'll never get anything done if we wait for consensus," Jamison said gently. He was holding Liza's hand. Even though she looked furious, she wasn't arguing anymore. He gave Dev a nod.

Dev followed Jamison to the door, shrugging on his coat as he went. He looked back once at Sarah. Her face was a storm of fury, but she didn't say a word, so Dev followed Jamison into the mudroom. There were two bullet holes in the siding of the house. One had come through the window of the storm door before Liza and Sarah had a chance to close it. The second had sliced through the bottom aluminum portion of the storm door and into the wall of the mudroom.

Dev tried not to think too deeply about how close Liza and Sarah had been to those bullet holes—and how there'd been nothing to do to get them inside any quicker except shoot back in the general direction of where the original shots had come from.

"Head for where the shots came from first?"

"Surely he's moved on from there," Jamison said. He had his gun in his hand, gaze sweeping the vast landscape in front of them. The rolling hills of the ranch were brown this time of year, dotted with patches of snow from the last accumulation they'd had.

"Unless we hit him." Dev hoped to God they had. Let this be over. Now.

Jamison grunted, which wasn't an argument, so they headed for the stables. Dev looked around for anything off. Shells, debris of any kind. A footprint in the patches of snow. Anything that shouldn't fit the normal day-to-day of the ranch.

Nothing out of the ordinary...except a sound. He and Jamison stopped, ears straining.

"It sounds like...scratching," Dev said. Then he broke out in a run, though it jarred his bad leg. He made it to the back of the stables, and then there was a bark. It was coming from the old chicken coop that hadn't been used in years.

"How the hell did Cash get in there?" Jamison muttered, jogging with Jamison to the old coop. Someone had used an old pipe to latch the door closed. Dev supposed he should be relieved whoever had been out here hadn't hurt Cash.

Dev pulled the pipe out so the door swung open. Cash flew out, snarling and barking. He darted off due north and Jamison and Dev exchanged a glance.

"I guess we follow."

Dev nodded, pointed at the shells littering the ground on this side of the stables. "This was his shooting point. Then he ran away?"

Cash darted back, then ran off again, the barking becoming more frenzied. The darting becoming more insistent. Quietly, gun tight in hand, Dev followed. They wouldn't sneak up on anyone with Cash losing it like this, but they didn't have a choice.

Dev and Jamison stopped on a dime at the top of a small rise of land. The grazing pasture stretched out before them, but not far off was a body. A very still, facedown-in-the-dirt body.

Dev started forward, but Jamison grabbed his arm and stopped him. "Could be a trap."

Dev gestured around. "We can pretty much see everything. Cody will check out the trees over there when he drives in, but that's too far away to get any good shot off on us—even with a high-powered weapon."

Jamison frowned, but he let go of Dev's arm and together they started forward. They took careful steps, guns at the ready, eyes trained around them until they reached the lifeless body. There was a gun still in the man's hand, but there was also a piece of paper pinned to the back of his shirt.

"It's set up just like my note," Jamison said, crouching to get a better look. Dev kicked the gun out of the lifeless man's hands.

"'Mike Christopher,'" Jamison read aloud. "'Crimes: armed robbery, battery, second-degree murder, but most of all—failure. Sentencing: death by firing squad.' Signed AW."

"Hardly a firing squad," Dev muttered. There was one bullet hole and it was clear the shot had been close range.

"Anth thinks he's judge, jury and executioner," Jamison said, looking away from the body and around them as if he could see something that would make any of this make sense.

"Then why did he send someone else to kill you?" Dev crouched too and studied the paper. It was typed like Jamison's, and set up exactly the same. Sort of like a court document, but more informal.

"Kill my family, you mean. That gunshot was meant for Liza."

But the more Dev thought about it, the more he wondered. Idly he petted Cash, who'd finally come to sit next to them now that he'd led them where he wanted them to be. "I'm not so sure it was meant for anyone. Maybe it was just to scare us. To scatter us like this." Jamison looked around them. No sign of another soul. "He sure didn't give this guy much of a chance. He got off two shots—then got murdered for his trouble."

"I think that means he didn't hit his target, Dev." Jamison stood, pulling his phone out of his pocket. "I'll call County. They'll want to do their own investigation, and get the ME to take the body."

"Sure," Dev agreed. Something about this was off to Dev, but that didn't mean more eyes trying to figure it out was a bad thing. "Good boy," Dev murmured, giving Cash a scratch behind the ears. "I bet we can even convince Grandma Pauline to let you sleep inside tonight." They'd need the extra lookout, because one thing was for sure.

This wasn't over. It was only the beginning.

Chapter Nine

The house was even more crowded now, though Sarah had to admit it helped her nerves feel less…frayed, she supposed. She was still nervous and scared. She kept thinking every little unexpected noise was a gunshot, but there was always someone to talk to or a kid or dog to play with.

The local police came and Jamison and Dev headed outside with them to show them all they'd found. Liza, Nina and Gage went upstairs to put their girls to bed. Once the police had finished their investigation and the removal of the body of the man who'd shot at them, Brady and Tucker drove out to the reservation to pick up Cecilia.

There was no more arguing, and no one tried to go off on their own. The aftermath was subdued.

Sarah was dead on her feet, and she knew she should go upstairs and sleep while she could. But she couldn't make herself leave the kitchen when Dev and Jamison hadn't come inside yet.

"They'll be in soon enough," Duke said gruffly from where he sat next to Grandma Pauline, working on a puzzle. They both had their reading glasses on and Sarah wanted to be amused, to feel cozily, Christmasy happy.

Instead she was jittery and anxious and...

She heard the outer door creak open, followed by the sound of stomping feet. When Dev and Jamison stepped inside, they'd shed their coats, but snowflakes still clung to their hair and Dev's beard.

Dev frowned at her. "I sure hope you're planning on cooking that baby a while longer. Roads are going to be a mess tonight."

"That is the plan."

"If Brady doesn't get back, you're full out of luck on the emergency medical personnel."

"I wasn't really planning on your brother delivering my baby, EMT training or no. And if you're trying to make some point about me staying in town—"

"I'm not trying to make any points. I'm just saying," he grumbled.

The kitchen descended into an uncomfortable silence. All eyes were on them and Sarah felt suddenly... see-through. Which was silly. They were always bickering. There was nothing weird about this to garner *looks*.

"I'm going to run through the shower," Dev muttered, moving into the hallway back to his room. Sarah watched him go until Jamison cleared his throat.

"Police took everything they could find. They'll be investigating. We've got an unmarked car on the road watching, but that's all they could spare. I know him though. We'll still want to have lookouts all night. A lot of ways to get on the ranch without using the road."

"Felicity came up with a schedule, but I don't think anyone will be sleeping until Brady, Cecilia and Tucker are back. Except this one here." Grandma Pauline pointed to Sarah.

"Go to bed, Sarah. Get some sleep," Jamison said gently. "We've got plenty of lookouts."

She should. She was *exhausted*. These were the last few days of having the luxury of just going to sleep when she wanted. "All right," she said, even though her easy agreement clearly shocked everyone in the kitchen. She gave Duke a hug and Grandma Pauline a shoulder squeeze and left the kitchen.

Much like earlier in the day, when she got to the stairs, she stood at the bottom and dreaded the uncomfortable climb. She could hear the shuffle of feet upstairs, the hushed murmurs of parents hoping their children were asleep.

She looked down the hall. She was going to be that parent soon enough. Whether the danger was over or it kept going for weeks. She was still going to be mom. And Dev wanted to be a father.

It was a huge step. One she should be happy about—satisfied with. But Sarah didn't know how to sit back and *accept* when there was so much more to have.

So, why stop now? Danger or no, life didn't stop. Maybe it had to pause for horrible threatening notes and gunshots, but she didn't have to let that stop her completely. Besides, what if something terrible *did* happen and she hadn't gone after everything?

She marched down the hall. She could hear the sound of the shower running in the tiny closet of a bathroom closest to Dev's room. She passed that door then stepped into Dev's bedroom.

It was also tiny. Sparse.

Grandma Pauline had groused about giving the dog special treatment, but she'd relented…and even let Brownie join Cash inside. Brownie was probably up in the girls' room being petted into oblivion. But Cash had settled onto Dev's bed and thumped his tail happily as Sarah walked in.

Sarah settled herself on the bed in the most comfortable sitting position she could manage. Cash put his head in her lap and she stroked his ears. It was calming, to the point she found herself nodding off. Every time her head drooped, she jerked back awake.

After who knew how many times of that, she jerked awake and Dev was standing in the doorway in sweatpants and a T-shirt. His feet were bare and his hair was wet and he was still holding a towel. He was staring at her with his perpetual scowl.

Her heart stumbled in her chest the way it always did when he caught her off guard.

"What are you doing?" he demanded gruffly.

Sarah stifled a yawn and sat up straighter. "Waiting for you."

He scrubbed the towel against his wet hair. "Why?"

"We didn't finish our conversation earlier."

There was a slight pause before he stepped fully

into the room. "We did finish it. I told you I'd be involved with the baby. The end." He stalked over to his dresser and jerked open a drawer.

"That's one part of it."

He pulled out a sweatshirt. "It's all parts of it."

"What I'll never understand about you, Dev, is you thinking I'm ever going to sit back and agree with your gruff declarations when I feel differently. You know I'm going to sit right here and poke at you until you have the conversation I want to have."

He stood completely still and didn't say anything, his back to her. She supposed because he knew she was right. She was who she was, and that wasn't a pushover or someone afraid to speak her mind.

If he didn't like that about her he was just going to have to come out and tell her point blank.

He dropped the towel in a laundry basket and pulled the sweatshirt over his head in quick, jerky movements. "I don't know what you're trying to get at. You wanted me to be involved, with the baby or… didn't care if I was or whatever—"

"I wanted you to be," Sarah said, all those emotions crashing around inside of her making her voice crack. "I want you to be involved."

"Okay, fine, great. So, you got your way. And we're friends. What more do you want?"

She frowned. If she thought he was being deliberately obtuse she would have been really mad, but he seemed actually baffled. "I want… I just think there could be more."

"We're friends," Dev said firmly.

"We had to be more than friends to make this baby."

"No. We had to be really drunk to make this baby. And you had to be really, really persistent."

"Dev." She slid off the bed. Her heart hammered in her chest. She could poke at him, and usually get her way, but this was more than getting her way. It was being honest. It was laying herself out for rejection.

Because truth be told, all the things she felt for him, she wasn't certain he reciprocated. Why had she avoided it all this time? Because she didn't know if Dev could ever look at her and see something other than an annoying neighbor who was slightly helpful with the whole ranching situation.

But that meant she didn't know if he *could* feel something for her. Or did. The only way to know was to put herself out there.

She considered getting up and going upstairs and leaving it at that. It would keep everything the way she was comfortable with, and wasn't that important when there was a madman threatening them and shooting at them?

But she found herself stepping forward, even as Dev stilled and looked down at her with that unreadable expression. She swallowed at her dry throat and lifted her hand to his cheek. He kept staring at her and nothing changed.

But he didn't step away. He didn't take her hand off his face. She wanted to do more. Press her mouth to his like she had back home. Hug him until something made sense and the fear melted away.

For so long she hadn't let herself feel this. She'd pushed it away. Prodded at him when what she'd always wanted to do was…this. Be there for him. Help him. *Love* him.

"I think there could be an us," she said, though her voice sounded strangled and her heart was beating so hard in her ears she could scarcely hear herself.

"Why the hell would you want there to be an us?" he asked, his voice ragged with pain. Then he stepped away from her hand and locked it all down. "We argue all the time. I'm old and grumpy and my leg doesn't work right," he said, his voice flat, his reasons just as flat.

The only way she'd ever figured to get through that shield of his was to be infuriating. "So?"

He curled his fingers in his hair like he was tempted to pull it out. "Go to bed, Sarah."

"Give me one good reason. All those things you listed? They're things I know about you. Have worked beside and cared about for most of my life. Your grumpy doesn't scare me. I don't care how many years older you are, and your reasoning is pretty bad if you're using your leg as an excuse."

"I am the son of Ace Wyatt, damn it."

He said it as if that was supposed to shock her. Or change her mind. When it was just another fact in a long line of them she'd always known. "Well, I'm the half sister of Anth Wyatt, apparently. I don't know what that has to do with anything."

"Why do you have to be such a steamroller?"

"It's the only way to get what you want."

"You don't know what you want."

"*You* apparently want me to punch you again." This time when she moved to touch him, it wasn't gently. She grabbed his forearms—to keep him there, to keep him still, to keep him connected. "If I was worried about the Wyatt blood, I wouldn't have badgered you into doing this for me. If I was worried about that… I can't even imagine. I never knew anything about my parents before this week. Not one thing. I told myself I didn't want to. Because it doesn't matter. They weren't in my life. I wish they'd had a chance to be, but… I had Duke and Eva. You had Grandma Pauline and your brothers. *That's* what matters."

"You always had Duke and Eva. I had the Sons. For years."

"So, I suppose Jamison is bad news. After all, he spent eighteen years with the Sons. And this baby? Tainted. Your blood's in there, Ace's too. Doesn't stand a chance, does he?"

"That isn't what I'm saying," Dev said, his teeth gritted.

"Then what *are* you saying?" She had to swallow at the lump in her throat. If he said he didn't feel that way—if he came out and truly rejected her—she would have to accept it. She would have to accept it and still allow his help raising the baby because she wanted him to be a father. He was still her partner in ranching. If he rejected her, she didn't get to run away or cut him out. He was always going to be here, and she'd have to suck it up and deal.

This was why you kept your stupid feelings to yourself.

But she remembered that he'd kissed her. Even if the aftermath was fuzzy. In that hotel hallway he'd kissed her. They'd made a baby together. When she touched him, he didn't bolt.

He settled.

There was something here. But it was Dev, so the only way to get to it was to fight for it. "You want to prove there's nothing here or it wouldn't work or whatever it is you're looking to prove—fine. Prove it. Kiss me."

SHE'D NEVER KNOW how for a split second Dev had been all too tempted to do just that—to shut her up, to stop this obnoxious, circular conversation, but most of all to have his arms around her.

She'd been shot at. Pregnant with his child and shot at because of her connection to him—more or less. He wanted to hold her and he wanted...

So many things he couldn't want. "Sarah." The problem was coming up with the words to get it through to her that this couldn't happen. *She* didn't want it to happen. Not really. Not for the right reasons.

"It's simple," she said, her voice maddeningly calm and her expression heartbreakingly vulnerable. Like she was laying her heart in his hands. "Kiss me. Prove there's no chemistry. We're just friends. Kiss me and prove there's *nothing* there."

He wished he could, but he remembered their night together all too well. There were all *sorts* of things there. But she was... She was Sarah, and he was him.

Which was not good enough. Plain and simple. It had nothing to do with Ace and everything to do with him.

He wasn't noble. He wasn't brave. He was a failure at all the things Jamison had tried to teach him to be when the Sons had been their lives.

Sarah slid her hands up his arms and linked her arms around his neck.

His body was a traitor, because it took all the will-power in all the world not to wrap his arms around her in return. A world of grit not to sink into what she wanted to prove. But he had to be stronger. For the both of them. For the *three* of them.

Eventually she'd realize she'd made a mistake. Maybe she would with him and the father thing too, but… A kid deserved a father who'd fight for him, even if he wasn't the best guy around. But Sarah…

She deserved the world. So he had to be a jerk. "I can be your friend and think you're hot and not have it mean anything."

She smirked up at him, arms still tight around his neck. "If you think I'm hot and it doesn't mean any-thing, then you can kiss me and it won't mean any-thing."

She wouldn't let this go. Didn't he know her? She didn't let anything go.

So, he'd have to somehow steel himself against it. Prove what he wanted to prove out of sheer force of will. Give her a bad, nothing kiss so she'd walk away understanding there was *nothing* here.

But of course the minute his mouth touched hers, he couldn't remember what he was supposed to be proving. He couldn't think past *her*. He was no saint. There was no nobility in him. One touch and he wanted more. One kiss and he wanted it all.

She opened up for him, just like she'd done at the hotel after the wedding. She wasn't drunk now, but she reacted all the same. As if this feeling had always been there, waiting underneath the surface.

He kissed her deeply, holding her tight against him. The evidence of their one night there between them, but that only made him want more. Want it all over again.

She'd said she didn't remember, but he remembered every minute, and it had tortured him for approximately nine months. To know everything could be that good, that hot, that *right* with someone who was supposed to be his friend, his business partner. The *girl* next door.

Not all this.

She slid her hands underneath his shirt, spreading her palms across his chest. He wanted to do the same, but...

He pulled his mouth from hers, though his arms stayed locked around her. "We have to stop." Had to. This was insanity on three hundred different levels.

"Why?" Sarah murmured, her fingers trailing down to the waistband of his pants.

He grabbed her wrists before she managed to get there. Thank *God*. "My grandmother and your father are in the next room. Also my dog is watching."

She looked down at Cash and then back up at him. "Well, I'll give you the family in the next room excuse." Her smile widened. "I don't think you proved your point just now."

"So there's chemistry," he grumbled, somehow both irritated and aroused by her smugness.

"Excellent chemistry."

"There is a madman out there who wants to hurt me and my brothers. You were almost in the crossfire today." Before she could open her mouth to go on and on and on, he kept talking. Focusing on reality rather than the desperate *want* raging through him. "Sarah, if Anth knows you're connected to him, it's bad enough. If he knows you mean something to me—Liza was the target there today. Don't you think?"

She frowned, her shoulders slumping. "Well, yes."

"I can't have you be a target. Not now." He lifted his hands to rest on her belly. Felt the odd rippling movement of baby inside. "This has to wait."

She studied his face, blue eyes sharp and assessing. He'd always felt like she'd seen him better than anyone. She always seemed to know what to do or say…except when she set out to irritate him. He was beginning to realize they were all purposeful. The understanding and the irritation.

Often just what he needed even if he didn't particularly *want* whatever she was pushing him toward.

"You know waiting is just going to give me more opportunity to strengthen my steamroller."

He chuckled in spite of himself. "Yeah, I'm well aware."

She let out a gusty sigh. "All right. I'll be good."

He wanted his mouth on her, so he shoved his hands in his pockets. He didn't trust her fake innocent look at all. "My butt you will."

She grinned. "Goodish?"

He grunted.

She bit her lip and he blew out a ragged breath. He couldn't convince her he was the wrong guy. Yet. There was still time. Once the danger was over, yeah, she'd come at him even harder, but she'd have a baby. Surely that would open her eyes. Surely having a real-life baby to take care of would make her realize he wasn't up to the task.

If the thought broke his heart a bit, well, good. It would get him ready for the inevitable. "Go on now. Get some sleep. We don't know when more danger is coming. Better get it while you can."

She nodded, studying his face as if she could read all his thoughts. Still, she didn't say anything and eventually moved slowly to the door, but she stopped there before opening it. "Dev?"

"What?"

She paused, that awful vulnerability and openness crossing over her face. "I know exactly what and who you are. I've always known. It's never changed how I felt about you, or what I thought you were capable of. I thought maybe I couldn't reach that part of you— not that it wasn't there." Then she left.

I thought maybe I couldn't reach that part of you— not that it wasn't there.

Not always so confident and sure of herself. Not always a steamroller going after what she wanted. He rubbed at the pain in his chest, knowing that realization would haunt him.

Even when the present danger was taken care of, he'd have a whole lot more to tackle with Sarah. And his heart.

Chapter Ten

The sound of crashing glass had Sarah's eyes flying open. There'd been a scream, she was sure of it. She whipped the covers off her and struggled to get out of bed quickly. It had come from somewhere upstairs, but not here in her room.

Once she got up, she ran for the door. By the time she made it to the hallway, everyone upstairs was crowded around the door to Cody and Nina's room.

Liza pushed through. She gave Sarah's arm a quick squeeze. "Everything's okay but I'm going to check on the girls."

"What happened?" But Liza had already moved down the hall to where the girls were sleeping.

Sarah grabbed the nearest person since she couldn't get close to Nina and Cody's door.

"A brick. Through the window. No one's hurt," Jamison said grimly.

A brick.

"Now, now. We aren't going to solve anything standing here with no room. Let's go downstairs and talk this through," Grandma Pauline ordered. She started shooing people down the hall.

Sarah backed up into her bedroom doorway as everyone who'd been upstairs started to file down the hall and to the stairs, including the dogs. Sarah moved to obey, but Dev crested the stairs. He patted Grandma Pauline's shoulder and headed for Cody and Nina's room.

Sarah followed him. He'd had his boots on, which Sarah realized was purposeful when he walked through the glass. Nina was still in bed, and Cody was standing next to it.

Dev carefully picked up the brick. He pulled a rubber band off of it, shook out the piece of paper wrapped around it, then handed it to Cody.

Cody's expression got even more grim. "I guess I've got my sentencing," Cody said.

Nina made a noise and Sarah thought about moving to offer some support, but there was window glass all over the floor and her feet were bare.

"Grab us some shoes out of the closet?"

Dev nodded and went to the closet. He pulled out pairs of shoes for Cody and then Nina and handed them over. Cody and Nina slid the shoes on in silence.

"We'll need to clean this up, but let's all go downstairs and talk things through first, yeah?"

Nina nodded, and she and Cody slid their arms around each other. Sarah moved out of the doorway again as Cody and Nina exited.

As Dev came out, he rubbed his hand over his beard before looking down at her. "You could go back to bed," he said, gently enough she didn't bristle. "It's the middle of the night. Nothing changes if you go back to bed."

"He knows what rooms we're sleeping in, Dev."

Dev expression went lax. He looked stricken, as though that hadn't occurred to him yet.

"The brick went through Cody's window and the paper was for Cody. None of us are safe in our rooms."

He swallowed and then slid his arm around her shoulders and started leading her to the stairs. "Okay, you're right."

It was the first time he'd admitted she was right and she couldn't take any pleasure in it. When they got downstairs everyone was in the kitchen, and the dogs were settled under the table, making Sarah think no one was still outside. Grandma was already reheating leftovers even though the clock said it was three.

"We didn't see anything," Cecilia said. She was sitting at the table, frowning at her hands.

Brady put his hand over hers. "None of the security lights went off. We were awake and paying attention. I didn't hear anything. I didn't… There was no warning."

"He's probably cut those too," Cody replied, his voice eerily calm as he encouraged Nina to sit down. "If he got the cameras, why not the motion sensors? I keep trying to rewire, add new passwords, but he cuts through all the tech. I hate to admit it, but I'm out of my league here."

Nina reached up and put her hand over Cody's on her shoulder. "We can't think of everything. It's impossible in a situation like this."

Dev nudged Sarah into an empty chair, then stood behind it. Grandma Pauline put a mug of hot tea in front of her. Duke paced the kitchen, and Jamison stood by the kitchen sink, looking out the window, as if he could see anything in the dark.

Liza was still upstairs with the kids, but everyone else was sitting around the table.

"Well, what does it say?" Duke demanded. "Just like Jamison's?"

Cody looked down at the paper. "Same setup. Slightly different wording."

Cody Wyatt
Crimes:
   The subject has been the perpetrator of a wide variety of crimes since childhood, but the most egregious of these is his involvement with the terrorist North Star Group. Murder, kidnapping, treason, terrorism.
Sentencing:
   For these acts, I do hereby sentence Cody Wyatt to death. This will be meted out at the judge's discretion through the method C. Wyatt deemed acceptable through his own connection to the terrorist group.
—AW

"Terrorist group," Cody muttered. "What a bunch of bull."

"It makes sense though," Sarah offered. "If you

look at it from his standpoint. North Star's mission was to take down the Sons. That's terrorism. To them."

"I don't understand where an affiliation with the Sons would come from if he was never *in* the Sons," Dev said, not dismissively but thoughtfully as though he were trying to work it out.

"But he was involved with Ace. Which means there could have been areas of the Sons he was involved in. We just don't know enough to make that assumption. But if he's blaming Cody for his work with North Star, and North Star's work was taking down the Sons, there has to be *some* connection."

"We only arrested Ace because of Cody and North Star's help," Jamison said. "It connects to Ace, even if it doesn't connect to the Sons. He's not going in age order with these letters. Or escape order. He's going in order of our involvement with Ace as adults. How did Ace going to jail start? With me helping Liza get Gigi out of the Sons. Which led us to the trafficking ring. Cody's North Star group was taking out their main guys, and the two of us coming together on that is what sent Ace to jail."

"I could have killed him," Cody said flatly. "I didn't."

"We have to remember we don't know what Ace told Anth," Sarah said. "We can only operate on what we know, but Ace could have told Anth *anything*. Truth or lie or a combination of both."

"But if he let Dev go all those years ago, helped Dev escape being killed by Ace, why would he... Why?" Liza said.

"Helping me escape doesn't have to mean he's

good. I think the past twenty-four hours proves he's not. We know the games Ace liked to play. This is another game. I think it also proves it isn't sudden. Anth has been planning this out for a while. Maybe since Ace died."

It was a terrible thought. If he'd had that long to plan, how could they win?

IT WAS A long night. It took a while for the girls to settle back down, and a while to clean up the mess of the glass. No one was too keen to go back to sleep in their rooms, but Dev convinced Sarah to lie down in his since there was no window. Felicity, Liza and Nina were all in the girls' room though he doubted with the cramped quarters and worried minds anyone was getting any sleep.

His brothers certainly weren't. They had someone at every entrance point on the lower level. Dev couldn't help but think the brick had been meant to scare them more than anything—a reminder AW could reach them whenever and however.

"How would he know which rooms we're sleeping in?" Dev wondered aloud. Dawn was beginning to break outside the large living room window he was guarding. Cody was leaning against the front door, eyes trained out the small sidelight window.

He looked exhausted. They probably all did. Another thing Anth likely wanted.

"No idea."

"It's weird though. Not just your average weird. With all of us here, we're not following any normal plan. Duke and Sarah never spend the night here, so there's no protocol to follow. Only the kids are in the room they're usually in, and he didn't go after them."

"Thank God," Cody muttered. "He touches my daughter, I won't be responsible for my actions."

"So, how? How did he know which room you and Nina were going to be in? How did he know to throw the brick in that window?"

"Could be a coincidence."

"Doubt it."

"I do too." Cody sighed. "There'd be no floor plan on file. The ranch isn't ever empty enough for a break-in, and like you said, we're not using our normal rooms anyway. I guess he could have planted a bug? But it's not like we talked about what rooms we're going to be in."

"No, and I don't think he can hear us. If he could… I feel like there'd be…more. He's cutting through your tech, but maybe that's because he's had time to figure it all out."

Cody nodded. "I can put up new stuff, but it'll take time. All the tech we've got involves the outdoors. The cameras, the lights—they're outside. He can't get in, or hasn't tried to, but he's messed with what's outside. He can't *hear* us in here, but what if he can see us?"

"What? Like X-ray vision?"

"No. No." Cody clapped his hands together. "Like my cameras. Not just taken out but rewired. Repurposed."

"That's possible?"

"It's *possible*. Especially if he's had so much time

to plan." Cody stepped away from the door. "It's getting light out. Watch my back while I—"

"You can't go out there. You're a specific target."

"I'm just going to check the cameras on the porch here."

"No, you're going to sit tight." Dev gave one last scan of the front yard he could see from the window, then strode for the kitchen. Gage was at the back door and Tucker was looking out through the window over the sink. "Cody thinks he might be getting our locations from the cameras and wants to go out and check."

"I don't think anyone should go out now that it's light," Tucker said.

"But if we can figure out how he knows what rooms we're in, isn't it worth the risk?" Gage replied. He stomped on the floor three times, a sign for Jamison to come up from the basement.

After a few seconds, Jamison stuck his out of the doorway into the basement. "See anything?"

"Cody thinks Anth might have tampered with the cameras and that's how he's getting an idea of where we are. He wants to go check it out."

"Not alone," Jamison said resolutely.

"We're trying to figure out how."

Jamison nodded. "All right. We'll have to assess. Together. Block all the doors except the one Cody wants to go out."

"What about windows?" Tucker asked.

"Close the curtains for now. If it's going to take too long we'll put lookouts back in place." They all moved to use the kitchen chairs as door barricades, then went to the front, where Cody was still looking out the door's sidelight, both dogs whining at his feet.

"I don't need to be out long. I'll just pull the camera off and bring it inside and see if I can find any evidence of tampering."

Dev didn't like it and knew none of his brothers did either. "I should do it."

"You don't know anything about cameras. No offense, but none of you do. I installed it. I can uninstall it quicker than any one of you."

"He could be hoping to draw you out of the house with that letter, Cody," Jamison replied.

"If he's sending letters to you then me, he's going to eventually send them to all of us. We're all targets. We're all in danger. I want to end that as soon as possible. I'm going to go out there and pull the camera off. It'll take me two, three minutes tops."

"Plenty of time to get shot," Gage muttered.

"I'll shield him," Dev said.

"Damn it, Dev."

"You can't be watching your back while you're uninstalling. You need at least one other person out there to be the eyes while you get it off the porch."

Cody couldn't argue with that, though Dev could tell he wanted to. "I could take the dogs."

Dev looked at Cash and Brownie. They were good ranch dogs, but... "They can't fight. They could easily be picked off. In fact, I think it'd be best if we get them off the ranch for the time being. Them going in and out for bathroom breaks is a liability."

"I agree," Tucker said. "But one thing at a time. Dev will watch north and east, I'll watch south and west. You guys will watch from in here. If we've got five sets of eyes on the situation, we'll be able to abort or defend ourselves."

All the brothers paused and looked at Jamison. It didn't seem to matter how old they all got, or how many times they'd saved people or themselves on their own, Jamison was their leader. He'd gotten them out of the Sons, and even now they'd seek his approval.

He gave a slight nod. So Dev immediately got to work. They switched weapons, giving Dev and Gage shotguns and Jamison and Brady the rifles.

"You move quick and quiet. The second you've got that camera off, you're back inside with Dev and Gage right behind. Jamison, hold the dogs."

They all nodded in affirmation. Dev went out first, watching the north and east side of the property they could see, immediately followed by Gage. Cody brought up the rear, keeping his eyes and focus on the camera.

Dev hadn't been a police officer for over a decade now, and it wasn't often that he missed it. He'd only gone into law enforcement to be like Jamison, and maybe to prove there was some goodness in him. Rancher was a better fit, though. He could understand and admit that now.

Today there was something bittersweet about being the protector, working side by side with his brothers to defend.

Dev didn't see anything, and based on the silence around him, Gage didn't either.

"Got it," Cody said after a while, and they all moved back inside as one unit.

Jamison pulled the door closed behind them and they huddled around Cody and the black box that housed the camera. He examined the wires, popped the back wall off and looked inside. He shook his head.

"It hasn't been tampered with," Cody said in disgust. "There weren't even any lines cut. Whatever blocking he did… I can't figure it out."

"Maybe it's not this camera," Dev said. "You have how many? And where are they?"

"There was the one on the front. I've got one on the stable that scans the entranceway. Then I've got three on the fence line. One at the gate, one on the west side of the house, and one on the south side of the property."

"West side of the house. Which way is that one facing?" Tucker asked.

"Toward the Knight property." Cody swiped his hand over his mouth. "But if it were moved, it could look into the west windows of the house."

"The only window on the west side is…" Jamison trailed off and they all rushed for the stairs. The only window was a long, narrow one at the end of the hall. Daylight was growing brighter, though everything was still dim. Still, Dev could see the small black box that would denote it was one of Cody's cameras.

"That where it's supposed to be?" Dev asked.

Cody's expression was barely banked fury. "Yes, but it isn't facing the Knight Ranch. It's facing us."

Dev caught a glimpse of something glinting in the rising sun. Even before he fully realized what it was, he was dropping to the floor and pulling as many brothers as he could with him. "Down!" Dev shouted.

They all hit the floor as the glass shattered above them.

Chapter Eleven

Sarah woke once again to the sound of a bang and shattering glass. At first she thought it had been a nightmare, just a replay of what had happened hours earlier. After all, they'd covered the bedroom windows where people were sleeping. She was in Dev's room, so there was no window here.

Surely it had been a nightmare.

But the dogs were barking like crazy and there were footsteps rushing above. Then her door opened and Dev moved inside. Before he even spoke she knew it wasn't a nightmare.

"Stay where you are."

"What? What's happened?"

"Another shot fired at the house. The six of us were together when it happened. Then we split up to tell everyone to stay put."

"More shooting at the house?" Her brain was sluggish and she tried to remember everything that had happened in the middle of the night. Too much, and this wasn't good. "Is everyone okay?"

"We're all fine. Jamison called the guy who was

on patrol and he's on his way, but I don't think he's going to find anything."

"What are we going to do?"

"I just need you to stay put for the time being. Once Jamison gets the all clear, we're going to go out ourselves and see if we can find a clue."

"You shouldn't go out." She flung the covers off her with the thought to jump out of bed and grab him, but he stalked over to the bed and pulled the covers right back over her.

"Stay put like I said," he ordered.

"You guys can't go out there. We are being *shot* at. You have to stay inside and…"

"And what? We have a ranch to run. You have a doctor's appointment today. We can't stay shut up inside hoping he goes away."

Sarah felt like crying. Of course the cattle couldn't be ignored. It wasn't smart to skip the doctor's appointment when she was this close to her due date. But didn't the people she loved outweigh all that?

He sighed and sat on the very edge of the bed. After a minute of clear internal debate, he took her hand and gave it a squeeze. "No one's been hurt. There are threats, and obviously this is scary, especially with you pregnant and the girls here, but we're handling it as best we can."

"We are sitting ducks."

He held her hand between his much bigger ones. There was some comfort in that, but not enough to soothe any of the fears. Twice they'd been shot at, and maybe the fact no one had been hurt meant something, but bullets flying around weren't ever a good thing.

"He'll make a mistake. He can't keep lurking around and not get caught."

"Why not? We live in the middle of *nowhere*. He's taken out almost all of Cody's security measures. He could lurk all day and all night and we'll never be able to do anything about it."

"I think at some point the five law enforcement officers living under the same roof means something."

She wished that comforted her any. It should. The Wyatt brothers were smart. Tucker was a detective so he was used to putting together clues and cases like this.

But so far, Anth was winning. He had the upper hand.

"What if you go out there to take care of the cattle and he ambushes you? What if all these scare tactics are to keep us inside so he has us all in one spot to—"

Jamison knocked on the door frame, peeking his head in. "Cops are finished. Found the gun. Why don't you all come out to the kitchen so we can talk about our next steps?"

"We'll be out in just a second," Dev said.

Jamison disappeared and Dev let go of her hand. Next steps. What could they possibly do next except hunker down?

"Sarah. You want to panic, that's just fine."

"I don't want to panic. I'm not panicking!"

She caught the way he pressed his lips together, as though he was trying not to laugh or point out she sounded a heck of a lot like someone panicking.

"Oh, shut up," she muttered. She let him help her out of the bed and they walked into the kitchen where, once again, everyone was huddled around the table. Except Grandma Pauline and Liza, who Sarah assumed were upstairs with the girls.

"I called the officer who was out in the car at the entrance. He did a quick search and found the gun that shot at us," Jamison said. "It was lying in the snow. There are footprints. He's called in some backup and they'll take the gun to see if they can lift a print. They're following the footprints too, best they can, though I suspect the wind will erase the trail before they get anything out of it. With all of us out of commission while we're under threat, they're stretched thin as it is." Four of the six Wyatt brothers worked for Valiant County, and though it was a big county with a big department, losing four officers from active duty probably was pretty stressful.

"I should help."

Sarah opened her mouth to argue, to demand everyone stay put, but Dev gave a dismissive wave her way.

"I'll be back in time to go with you to your appointment."

The smart aleck response died before she could say it as she realized there were questioning looks around the room. Confusion. Except from Duke.

In all the craziness, Sarah hadn't fully thought about the fact Dev wanting to be a father to the baby would mean telling everyone. No one knew yet and it would be a whole…thing, in the midst of this other thing.

"I think you should go see your doctor too," Cody said to Nina, dragging people's attention away from Sarah and Dev. "It's just a little bit earlier than your normal appointment time. I don't see the harm in getting checked out. You can take Brianna and—"

"Separating us isn't going to do any good. If he wants me to get to you, then I'm a target too."

Sarah shook her head. There was a pattern, and maybe Anth could deviate from it, but why would he have a pattern if he wasn't using it for some reason? "Gage would be next," she said. "Anth sent a note to Jamison, then shot at Liza. Or had someone shoot at Liza. Then there was a note to Cody, and he shot at you guys. That's a pattern, and it means the next thing to happen would be for Gage to get a note, since he was the next one to have a run-in with Ace."

"Lucky me," Gage muttered as Felicity wrapped her arm around his.

"This is a North Star gun," Cody said, placing his phone in the middle of the table. On the screen was a picture of a gun in the snow. "The gun he used—it's from North Star. Or at least it's the kind we were issued. He could get his hands on it easy enough without going through North Star, but doesn't that feel…"

"Pointed?" Sarah supplied. "It connects to your note. Just like shooting at Liza connected to all the uses of kin in Jamison's note."

"But neither attempt succeeded at killing their target," Dev said thoughtfully, staring down at the picture of the gun.

"Maybe he doesn't want to succeed. Maybe this is the game."

"The paper says we're sentenced to death. Why would he sentence us to death, then play a game?"

"I don't know, but why take a shot at Liza? That doesn't kill you. Metaphorically, maybe. But are we dealing in metaphors? Maybe the letters and the attempts to hurt us aren't connected in the way we're thinking," Sarah insisted. "First it was Jamison, then Cody. If they're going in involvement with Ace order, like I said, Gage would be next. Some kind of attempt that connects to the note. Then a note for Brady."

"What Cecilia and I dealt with was Elijah, not Ace," Brady said. But Sarah could tell even though they were voicing arguments, what they were really doing was thinking it through. Working out the angles.

"Elijah was a protégé of Ace," Sarah continued. "Besides, you were involved with saving Gage from Ace even before that. So, either way, you'd be after Gage." Sarah looked at Tucker. "Ace didn't have too much to do with your showdown with the Sons, but he died while you were fighting them."

"It doesn't make sense, though," Dev said gruffly. "If it was about Ace, I would have been first. It would have gone back to me. It doesn't make sense to leave me for last."

"Maybe it doesn't have to make sense to us," Nina said quietly. "It makes sense to him."

Sarah couldn't help but think there was something they were missing. Some piece of the puzzle that would allow them to make sense of things.

"I'm going to go help them follow the trail. I'll notice things they won't."

"Not alone," Jamison said sharply. "Under no circumstances are any of us going anywhere alone."

"I'll go," Duke said, standing. "May not be as young as you lot, but I know how to shoot a gun and follow a trail. It's my land too."

Dev nodded and they both headed for the mudroom to get bundled up. When she stood, Duke gave her a censoring look. "Stay put." Then they headed outside into the snowy, cold morning.

Sarah scowled after them. She was very tempted *not* to stay put, but she was nine months pregnant. She couldn't go waddling around trying to track a killer. But what she could do was try to get to the bottom of the pattern. "I want to see the letters again. We need to compare them."

DEV FOLLOWED THE trail of boot prints in the snow that led from where the county cops had parked their car, to the place they'd found the gun. It had since been processed and taken in as evidence with the hope of lifting a print.

Dev had his doubts. Why would Anth—or someone Anth had hired—drop a weapon that might have fingerprints on it? Didn't make any sense.

Still, there could be something left behind. Some clue—either from the direction the trail went or something *accidentally* left behind. Something the cops might not know to look for.

"He isn't headed back to my house, and he isn't headed to the highway," Duke said from behind Dev. They were walking close together, eyes sweeping the wide-open spread of land between them.

"If the trail is headed to where he's going. Not sure he's that dumb."

"One way or another, we need this done before that baby comes along. You're running out of time."

Dev kept his sarcastic *no kidding* to himself. In an effort to not mess up the path the shooter had left, the police officers had ruined any secondary evidence Dev might have been able to pick up on. Necessary for them, but a shame for Dev.

He tried to focus on that. The footprints, what the path meant, and what he was looking for, but he could practically *feel* Duke's disapproval waving over him.

He shouldn't care. Duke's approval didn't matter. Maybe it had once upon a time, but Dev had given up on seeking approval after he'd ended up in the hospital, his law enforcement career over, and knowing he was a failure.

Utterly, in every way that mattered.

He'd eventually pulled himself out of that dark, self-pitying place. Or maybe more accurately, Sarah had poked him out of that place.

On purpose, he realized with a start. He'd always thought she was just annoying, but no. She'd gone about dragging him back into the land of the living since he'd been able to walk again.

She'd never given up on him, and never tipped her hand. She'd always known exactly what she was doing, but she'd never let him know. Probably because she knew he'd balk at it.

His chest felt too tight and now was not the time for after-the-fact realizations or emotions he didn't want to analyze. But he owed Duke something, because through Sarah's badgering and Grandma Pauline's calm presence and his own stubbornness, he'd pulled himself out of that ugly place. He wasn't perfect or maybe any good, but he'd put some pride in this ranch and his hard work here.

He'd made progress. Not just in the years, but maybe even in the months of Sarah's pregnancy. "I'm not going to...shirk my responsibilities with her. Well, with the baby," he said, half hoping the words died in the wind.

"Please tell me you didn't say it like that when you told her," Duke replied. "Well, you don't have a black eye so you must have phrased it better."

"Yeah, I phrased it better," Dev muttered. "I said I'd be a father. That I wanted to be. I... Someone who'd protect my kid no matter what. I guess you don't have to be perfect to do that."

"No, son. You don't. But it isn't just about protecting. Being a parent is so much bigger than that."

Dev stopped and rubbed at his aching leg. The cold exacerbated the pain and Duke's words had a clutching, crushing sensation rocketing through his chest. *So much bigger. You really think you can handle that?*

Too late to rethink. He'd said he'd be a father to the

baby, and he wouldn't go back on his word. Besides, there was no time to panic about the future when the present was just as ominous.

"Then there's being a partner to think about. You'll both have different ideas of how to raise the boy. Then there's your own relationship, which… Well, it's hard enough to make those decisions when you're settled and married. It's a balancing act. It's—"

"Is now really the time to lecture me on all the ways I'm going to screw it up?"

"No time like the present," Duke said. He almost sounded cheerful, but Dev supposed that's because he was distracting himself by trying to scare the bejesus out of Dev. "Besides, you'll both screw it up. That's the beauty of life if you think about it. Everybody makes mistakes, so it hardly makes yours the end of the world like you're so prone to do."

"I'm not prone to do that," Dev muttered. "Much." But before he could analyze how right Duke might be, his attention was drawn to a difference in the snow. There were still footprints here, but the snow was packed differently. He could see where the cops had gone on, following the prints.

But there was something off here, even if he couldn't figure out what. "Do you see this?"

Duke studied the snow too. "Something isn't right. Is it packed in?"

"Seems to be. But that's a heck of a lot of packing."

"Unless…" Duke trailed off, but he lifted a gloved hand and pointed a little ways off. After an area of packed snow, there were two indentations. Like snow-mobile tracks.

"Let's be careful where we walk," Dev said, starting to head that way and trying to avoid marring any tracks. After just a few steps, he saw a dark stain of red between the indentations. It was a narrow trickle following the path of the mobile.

Dev looked at Duke, who already had his phone to his ear. "Jamison. We found something. Don't know how far your deputy friends are ahead of us, but can you radio them back? They'll be able to see our trail and follow us."

Duke hung up and they kept walking.

"Better watch out for an ambush, boy."

Dev looked around. It was an open field. Though the land rolled a bit here and there, with the snow it would be almost impossible to hide.

The snowmobile tracks curved around a swell of land. Duke and Dev slowed in unison as they rounded the tiny hill. The red dribble of blood stopped behind the swell, where Dev could spot hair.

He held out an arm and stopped Duke, but Duke shook his head. "I don't think that's a live one."

Dev let out a breath and then they walked closer, the body coming more into view. He didn't recognize the man, though he was clearly dead. A giant arrow was coming out of his chest, and he didn't move. His unseeing eyes just stared at the bright sun above.

Attached to the body, via the arrow, was another piece of paper. Duke swore. Dev moved closer to read the note, being careful not to disrupt any more of the scene.

Craig Timothy
Crimes:
   Armed robbery, rape, first and second-degree murder, but most of all—failure.
Sentencing:
   Death by lethal injection.
—AW

"Seems to me a man with all these notes, who can disappear or send other people to do his dirty work, would choose people less likely to fail."

Dev would agree, but he thought about what Sarah had said. That this was just a game. Or maybe unrelated to the Wyatts. Maybe Anth simply wanted to get rid of these men for whatever reason, and this was the way to do it. Maybe he wanted to confuse them, or just scare them by showing them what he could do.

Too many options, but so much failure didn't make sense. It had to be planned. It had to be purposeful. Which put Dev even more on edge than he already was.

"Dev." Duke's voice was especially grave, and when Dev looked back at the man, Duke nodded toward the corpse's hand.

There was a folded up piece of paper, but clearly printed on the part Dev could see was his brother's name. Gage Wyatt. Just like Sarah had predicted.

"Let's go find the cops," Dev said grimly.

Chapter Twelve

By the time Dev and Duke returned to the house, Sarah had read and reread the notes left for Jamison and Cody. Now she had a third note to read. Gage, just as she'd predicted.

"Oh, allow me," Gage said when Dev said he was going to read it to everyone.

"It's just a picture. The cops took the original to see if they could lift some prints off it." Dev handed his phone to Gage. Felicity sat down, Claire squirming in her lap.

Sarah thought the way Claire was cheerfully babbling at Felicity helped ease some of Felicity's tension now that her husband received the specific threat.

"'Gage Wyatt. Crimes: The subject has been the perpetrator of a wide variety of crimes since childhood. Manslaughter. Battery. Treason. Escape from custody and sentencing. Attempted patricide.'" Gage smirked. "Hard to argue with that one."

"What's the sentencing?" Sarah encouraged him. They'd all followed the same lines, and the sentencing was always the clue to how they were going to be attacked.

"'Sentencing: For these acts, I do hereby sentence Gage Wyatt to death. This will be meted out at the judge's discretion through the method G. Wyatt saw fit to use on his own father.' Signed AW." Gage handed Dev his phone back. "Well, unless he plans on dragging me off to a cave somewhere, I think I'm safe."

"Don't say that," Felicity said. She'd gone more and more pale as Gage had read the note and his last little quip hadn't helped. But Felicity had been there when Ace had tied Gage up in a cave in the Badlands. She'd been the one to save Gage from Ace.

"It doesn't make sense anyway. I didn't try to kill him. *He* tried to kill *me*. Felicity is the one who shot him."

"We keep running into a lot of things not making sense," Dev said grimly. "I imagine we'll meet a few more before this is all over. We need to keep being diligent, but the current challenge is going to be getting Sarah to her doctor's appointment."

"The cops could take her. We could hide her, you know? Sneak her out to the cop car so no one who might be watching would even know."

"No," Dev said. "I'll be going."

The room went silent, those speculative glances they'd gotten earlier increasing with real interest. Sarah knew there was no way to avoid this. No matter the danger. Her family deserved to know and unless Anth Wyatt had planted some kind of listening device…

"You don't think we're being listened to, do you?" she asked Cody.

Cody shook his head. "I've swept this room in particular up and down and sideways. I can't find any evidence he can hear us. Him knowing which bedrooms we're in would have been easy enough to determine by watching through the camera he had pointed in the hallway window upstairs. I think if he could *hear* us, we would have been ambushed any of the times we've gone outside."

Sarah nodded, then shared a look with Dev. She didn't have to say anything for him to incline his head. A silent *go ahead.* "I'm going with Sarah because I'm the father."

There was nothing but silence at first. Even Duke was silent though he already knew. Everyone looked downright shocked, except maybe Grandma Pauline who'd always had an excellent poker face. Surely even *she* couldn't have predicted this news.

"As in..." Nina cleared her throat. "Like you're *actually* the father, or you're stepping in to play—"

"I'm *actually* the father."

Cecilia let out a gasping noise. "Oh my... You had sex at our wedding."

Sarah didn't consider herself someone who embarrassed easily or almost ever, but heat stole over her cheeks and she got the feeling she was bright red.

"I don't think we need to go into the details," Dev said dryly. "Now. It shouldn't be just the two of us. Nina, did you want to go in and get checked out?"

Nina shook her head as if needing the physical

movement to change topics. She cleared her throat again. "Right. Yes. Cody made an appointment for me, though it's later than yours." She shot her husband a disapproving look, but she'd placed a protective hand over her still-flat stomach. "But Cody should come too."

"I agree," Sarah said before Cody or Dev could argue. "We're all in this house because we believe there's safety in numbers. We should go to town and back in more than just a duo or a trio. Four is good."

"And a police escort," Jamison said authoritatively. "I've already talked to the department. The weather is stretching them even thinner, but they've called in some road help from neighboring departments. They've agreed the best course of action was to have a marked police car following you guys."

There were a few more practicalities, but before Sarah could really study Gage's note to her liking, she was being ushered out the door to head to her doctor's appointment.

Cody was driving, and they'd decided to take Brady's truck since he'd yet to get a note with his name on it. Though it was only a matter of time, it seemed smarter to avoid a vehicle specifically owned by someone who'd already been "sentenced."

Once Cody drove out onto the highway, a cop car pulled behind them. Following them toward town.

Sarah sat in the back with Nina, who she could all but *feel* studying her. Sarah didn't know what to say, so she kept her mouth shut.

Until Nina broke the silence. "You really...slept together?"

Sarah gave Nina a doleful look. "That *is* how babies are made."

"Why didn't you tell anyone? For *nine* months?"

Dev's gaze met hers in the rearview mirror. She didn't know what to say. Sure, she could give the truth. He probably wanted her to. But it wasn't exactly the whole truth, no matter how she'd convinced herself it was.

Turned out, with the actual possibility of Dev as a father to her child, as a partner, she could admit to herself she'd convinced herself of the insane plan because she'd hoped for this. She just hadn't dared *plan* for it.

"It's complicated," Dev said before she could think of what to say. "And we have a few more complicated matters to focus on."

Nina frowned at the back of his head, but she didn't press the matter. They finished the drive in tense silence, all eyes on the world around them as they drove. Wondering if something would jump out and harm them.

It was a terrible way to live. Sarah wished she could be *doing* something, but instead she had to walk into the medical building and wait for what felt like eternity to be led back to one of the exam rooms. There was the weighing, the peeing in a cup and then more waiting.

Dev looked large and uncomfortable in the small chairs in the exam room. He kept adjusting his weight.

"Honestly, you'd think *you* were the one nine months pregnant in a paper gown."

He glanced at her in the paper gown, then looked up at the ceiling. "You're not exactly covered up very well."

"That's because she's going to shove her—"

A knock cut off what Sarah had been going to horrify Dev with. The doctor stepped in, then stopped short at the man in the chair. "Well, hello. I'm Dr. Marks."

"Dev. Dev Wyatt." He shook the doctor's hand. "I'm the father."

"Well, lovely. Let's get started then, shall we? Everything looks good with your weight and blood pressure and sample. We'll do the heartbeat, then do an internal."

Sarah had to bite back a laugh at the way Dev paled. Her humor faded, as it always did, when the doctor put the monitor on her stomach and the quick, mechanical *womp womp* filled the room.

"Heart rate is good," the doctor said.

Sarah hadn't noticed Dev had come to stand beside her, she'd been so focused on the heartbeat. His fingers intertwined with hers and she looked up at him. There was sheer *awe* on his face—she knew because she felt it every time. But it was bigger, more emotional with him here to share it.

She hadn't come to these appointments alone. She'd always had one of her sisters insist on coming with. She'd always known she wouldn't raise this baby alone, but knowing she—or this baby—

had reached Dev and brought him here…where he could experience *life*. And wonder. And joy.

She wanted to cry, but she blinked the tears back.

"Now to check your cervix." Casually explaining what she was doing and why to Dev, the doctor went through the exam. When she was finished, she gave Sarah a sympathetic smile.

"No dilation. I think he's content to stay put for a while longer yet. We might even want to schedule an induction for after Christmas. We don't want him hanging out in there too long."

"Even with the contractions she's been having, you think he's going to stay put?"

The doctor smiled indulgently. "Anything is possible, Mr. Wyatt. She could have him tomorrow. But the likelihood of him coming early at this point is slim. First-time births are notoriously late and slow. She should have plenty of warning when he's coming."

"So, what you're saying is it's perfectly safe to stay out at the ranch through Christmas, even if the weather forecast is bad," Sarah said.

The doctor paused, looked from Dev's scowling face to Sarah. "Well. It'd be good to pay attention to the weather forecast. You wouldn't want to be caught too far away from a medical facility. But I think you're pretty safe as long as there aren't any more contractions. Considering how far you are from the hospital, I'd say you start getting regular contractions, even if they're pretty far apart, you'd want to make your way close. Especially if the weather is bad."

Sarah gave Dev a triumphant smile.

"If he's not here for Christmas, we'll see you back next week. I'm out of the office until the new year, but my nurse practitioner can check you out, and I'll be on call for any births. You both have a nice holiday. Take your time getting dressed."

Sarah thanked the doctor before she left. She needed Dev's help to get herself off the table. Getting undressed in front of him hadn't been that big of a deal because she'd had the paper gown to put over her before she'd shimmied out of her pants.

Now it was a little more awkward. Especially when he handed her her pants. Still, she felt more weird about asking him to turn around or close his eyes or something, so she twisted and turned to pull her pants back on while keeping the paper in place.

Of course, then she had to slide it off to put on her shirt, but that was... Well, her bra was no different than a swimsuit really.

Uncomfortable but unwilling to say so, she let the paper gown drop and took the sweatshirt Dev handed to her. But before she could pull it over her head, he placed his hands over her belly. His bare hands on her bare belly. "I can feel him kick you. I heard his heart beat. But he still doesn't feel...*real.*"

No, none of any of this felt real, most especially Dev touching her like this. But it would. At least the baby would. "He will. When you hold him. When he's here. It'll feel more real than we can imagine."

"You're so sure?"

"I watched Gage and Felicity. Pretty intently, since I was starting to hatch my plan then. So, yeah, I'm sure. Something changes when he actually gets here. Something big."

He looked at her then—*her*—not her belly. The gaze was searching. Open. There was something in those hazel eyes that had her breath catching in her throat.

But then he only dropped his hands and stepped back. "We should get going. Don't want to be separated any more than we have to be."

Sarah could only nod, because her throat was too tight, and everything she'd dreamed of was too close. But instead of reaching for it, demanding it, she kept her mouth shut and followed Dev back out to the waiting room where Nina and Cody were.

Because there was still a madman torturing them, and no dreams were going to be realized in the midst of that.

DEV KEPT EXPECTING something to happen, but they were back at the ranch by suppertime safe and sound. Not even the hint that anyone had followed, nor had anything new happened at the ranch while they were gone.

After supper, Sarah went to bed early. They'd agreed on four people staying awake for four hours, then another four people for the next, to get them through the night. Dev was on the first shift tonight.

He stood in the kitchen while his brothers said good-night to their kids and wives and people slowly settled into bed. He should be thinking about Anth. About the notes and sentences and the dead bodies.

But all he could think about was that doctor's office. He'd heard his child's heartbeat. An odd noise. Not really human. Not really…

It hadn't been magic. He didn't suddenly think he'd be some amazing father, or that Sarah didn't deserve better. Like he'd told her, it still didn't feel *real*. But it had touched something inside of him. Something he'd preferred to have left dead.

Life was easier that way. Easier without all this… this…

This.

But now that the Pandora's box was open, there was no shoving it back.

When Jamison, Cody and Gage all walked into the kitchen and instead of determining lookout posts, grabbed four beers from the fridge and handed him one, Dev blinked. "What's this?"

"The Dad crew," Gage said, clinking his bottle of beer to Dev's. "Welcome."

"I'm not a dad yet."

"Dad enough," Cody said with a grin. "The real terror is *just* beginning."

Dev shifted uncomfortably. "We've got actual terror to deal with first."

Gage laughed. "Buddy, you don't *know* real terror 'til that baby is crying at two in the morning and you ain't got a clue as to why."

"Or your eight-year-old looks up at you and says, 'Daddy, where do babies come from?'"

Gage snorted out a laugh at Cody's rendition of Brianna's high-pitched questions.

"We just wanted to congratulate you," Jamison said. "Whatever the circumstances that brought you here, being a father is… It's a big thing. It's a good thing."

Dev wanted to shrug away all that…emotion. Before his brush with death, he'd wanted to model himself after Jamison. Then he'd realized he was such a coward. He'd given up on that dream. So having any kind of Jamison's approval felt like a noose. "Maybe for the likes of you, but I'm pretty sure it's a terribly selfish thing for me."

"Selfish?"

"I wasn't going to be involved. Before you get that battle light in your eye, Jamison, Sarah didn't *want* me to be. Or at least, she said she didn't. But when all the danger started, I got to thinking about how we weren't protected when we were babies. We had each other, but we didn't have a parent who'd lay it all down to keep us safe and I just… I wanted to be that. Isn't that selfish?"

His brothers were silent and Dev wished he'd kept his big mouth shut.

"I think we can convince ourselves of a lot of things," Jamison said at length. "That we're the most selfish. Or the most noble. I think it's human nature to cast ourselves in some role—hero or villain. Maybe most especially when we grew up with nothing but villains."

That made a little too much sense to Dev, who'd often wanted to cast himself as the villain because… Well, he hadn't been as good as the heroes in his life.

But he hadn't been as bad as the villains in his life, had he?

"Maybe it's part selfish to want to give someone what you didn't have, but being a father isn't a selfish act. Giving isn't… It can be for selfish reasons, but it'll change you. Having that kid. It changed me and I didn't meet Brianna until she was seven."

"Gigi isn't mine in the biological sense of things," Jamison said carefully. "When you choose to be a father—when *we* choose to be fathers—I don't think you could ever separate what Ace was to us, did to us, from that choice. Maybe it's selfish, but… We're human. You can't separate your humanness from your relationships with other people—the ones you choose, the ones you don't. Life's complicated. It isn't black and white."

Gage clapped Jamison on the back. "My God, an old dog *can* learn new tricks."

"Ha. Ha," Jamison replied with an eye roll.

Before they could say anything more to make him feel…confused all over again, Liza walked into the kitchen.

"Everyone's down for the night pretty much. You guys are officially on lookout. But I just wanted to warn you not to play hero and not wake us up," Liza warned, and while Dev figured that warning was mostly for Jamison, she looked at all of them. "We're in this together. Always."

"I promise," Jamison replied.

Cody and Gage followed Liza out of the kitchen to their posts at the front of the house. Dev was assigned the kitchen window and door. Jamison was supposed to have the basement, but he stood there not moving for his station.

Dev shifted uncomfortably under his brother's assessing gaze. "What?" he demanded. "We had our little heart-to-heart. Now it's time to do our jobs."

But Jamison didn't stop looking at him like he understood all the horrible depths of his soul. He reached out and squeezed Dev's shoulder. "I don't think you've ever given yourself room to be human, Dev. You always wanted to be more or better, but sometimes being you is enough."

Dev didn't know how that could be true, but he also didn't know how to refute his oldest brother's words. And they hung with him as Jamison left for his post, as he spent four hours watching out. As he went to his room, where Sarah was asleep in his bed.

He didn't disturb her, rolling out a sleeping bag on the floor, but he couldn't sleep because Jamison's words haunted him. His own thoughts haunted him.

If he could be enough…what might the future hold?

Chapter Thirteen

Sarah was happy to wake up naturally, even if it was a bit late. She yawned and pawed on the nightstand for her phone. *Really* late. Almost noon. No one should have let her sleep that long.

She lumbered out of bed, winced a little at the pain in her stomach. Not like a contraction. More achy than sharp. Probably just slept on it wrong. Or just her muscles aching from all this *weight* she was hefting around.

She took care of practicalities and got dressed, wondering where Dev had slept and if she'd missed anything terrible happening. It would be nice to wake up and just...have a normal life again.

When she walked down the hall and into the kitchen, it was bustling. Almost like that normal life she'd wanted had showed up as ordered.

Of course, real life wasn't sleeping in Dev's bed or walking into Grandma Pauline's kitchen at nearly noon after having slept through chores, but it was nice nonetheless.

The two older children were at the table with a

variety of dishes. Claire was in her high chair banging happily at the tray. Grandma Pauline and Rachel were hunched over the counters, mixing together what looked like cookie dough.

"What's all this?"

"We're going to decorate for Christmas," Brianna said, bouncing in her seat. "Daddy and all the uncles went to get a tree!"

"And we're going to make cookies, and have hot chocolate tonight when we decorate," Gigi said, matching Brianna's excitement.

Sarah might have smiled at their enthusiasm, but Brianna's statement had her moving over to Grandma Pauline. She couldn't think of one time in her life where she'd dared question Grandma Pauline, but the words came out of her in a hissed whisper she couldn't bite back.

"We're being threatened and you sent them to cut down a tree?" It was usually a Christmas Eve tradition anyway. While at the Knight Ranch they'd had their tree up since the beginning of December, Grandma Pauline's family had always done it on Christmas Eve, and she was a stickler for tradition.

Until, apparently, danger was in the equation.

Grandma Pauline spared her one cutting look. "Christmas will come one way or another, Sarah."

Sarah felt chagrined, even though she shouldn't. "Yes, whether we put a tree up or not."

Grandma looked at the girls, happily browsing through bottles of sprinkles. "I suppose we should let this ne'er-do-well ruin their Christmas, hide in closets until the danger has passed…if it ever does. I suppose I should have never had a Christmas for those boys when Ace was always a threat."

Sarah didn't have *anything* to say to that, and she noted Rachel kept her head down over the counter.

"Those men are out doing chores, don't know why they couldn't cut a tree down all the same. You go on and sit yourself down."

Sarah didn't know what else to do but listen. In a few short minutes, Grandma had a lunch plate in front of her. A sandwich, a clementine and a handful of pretzels. Even worried about the men out chopping down Christmas trees, the gesture made her smile and feel ten years old again.

Sadly, she wasn't ten. A ten-year-old didn't need to worry about people's lives or her baby being born. Sarah rubbed a hand over her stomach. She choked down a few bites of her lunch, though she wasn't hungry at all.

She feigned interest in the Christmas decorations, but mostly she studied her phone, where she had pictures of all three notes. She read them over and over again, still sure there was a pattern just out of reach.

The men returned, all seven of them stomping and shedding their winter layers. They left the tree in the mudroom so they could scrounge up the stand and get that set up first.

Grandma had lunch plates put together in no time. Dev took a seat next to her and peered at her phone screen.

"Looking at it won't change it."

"No. It won't. But there's a pattern. There's a... reason. I can *feel* it. I just can't work out what it is."

"Maybe you should have been a cop. Some kind of detective."

"All those rules to follow?" She wrinkled her nose. "No thanks."

He smiled at her. An actual smile. Like he enjoyed her company or liked looking at her or *something*. It had a warmth warring with an odd jittery feeling that this was *all* wrong, even though it was what she wanted. What she'd always wanted.

Now it was here and she didn't quite know what to do with it. With him.

"Whichever two of you are done first go on down-stairs and get the decorations," Grandma Pauline said, still working on the cookie dough with Rachel. "They're in tubs in the crawl space."

Dev slid her phone away from her and she scowled at him. "Take a break. It's almost Christmas."

"Since when are you known for taking a break and enjoying Christmas cheer?"

"Well, I'm not, but I figure I'd start."

She felt a bit like the Grinch with a heart swelling too many sizes to possibly be healthy. With all that amazement and heart growing came this ever evolving fear that...well, a million things would go wrong.

Cody and Gage got up and headed for the basement as Grandma Pauline had instructed earlier. Sarah was distracted enough to return to her previous thoughts. Because as great as it was to have Dev here, wanting to be a father, wanting…something…it didn't matter until they were safe.

She wasn't sure she knew how to believe it was real until the danger was gone. Maybe it was all an act, or some kind of hysteria brought on by worry.

"If we could work it out, the letters, the pattern— maybe we could catch him in the act. Whether it's one of these attacks, or it's in leaving one of the letters. I know there's a connection."

"Until we know what it is, I'm not sure what we can do about it. He keeps cutting through all Cody's safety measures, and I took the dogs over to the Pullman Ranch until we know they won't get hurt in the crossfire."

"Brethren and North Star and caves," Sarah muttered, repeating the info from the letters. "Brady's standoff with the Sons was in the Badlands. So maybe—wait. Caves." She grabbed Dev's arm. "Crawl space. A crawl space is like a cave. Like Gage said. Anth could only hurt him if—"

Dev was already to the basement door. He yelled a sharp *stop* as he flew down the stairs. Sarah had to struggle to her feet. "I think there's something in the crawl space. I think—"

"It's a bomb," Dev yelled from the basement. "Get everyone out."

CODY BARKED ORDERS into his phone as they ran upstairs. Everyone who'd been in the kitchen was already filing out the door.

"Do we have everyone?" Cody asked.

"Yes. We made sure," Sarah answered. She had a handful of coats in her arms. Grandma Pauline and the girls were already long gone, and the rest of the Wyatts were trailing out behind them.

Dev took Sarah by the arm as they got to the mudroom. He didn't chastise her for still being inside, just pulled her with him as they hurried outside.

"Let's get away from the house. None of us know enough about bombs to know how much power that one could have."

"We need to get out of the elements," Liza returned. "We grabbed what boots and coats we could, but not enough for everyone to be out in the cold like this."

Liza was carrying Gigi. Brady had Brianna since she was too big for Nina to carry and Cody had been back with Dev. Felicity had Claire wrapped in someone else's coat. Duke had his arm linked with Grandma—and Grandma didn't even yell at him for treating her like an old lady.

"Head to the stables," Dev said. "That'll give us shelter." And cover if the explosion was particularly violent. It hadn't been a large device. Dev wasn't even sure he'd have thought it was a bomb if Cody hadn't been certain and Sarah hadn't thought the crawl space was dangerous and connected to the last letter. Still, who knew what kind of damage it could do? If they were in the stables, they'd all be together and the walls should protect them.

God, he hoped.

Dev's gaze swept the area around them. No sign

of anyone. No shots rang out. The move to the stables made him nervous, but there was no other choice with a bomb in the house.

Which could have been Anth's purpose.

Dev pulled open the stable door and ushered everyone inside. He double checked to make sure they had everyone, then closed the door.

The horses neighed and nickered. They weren't getting the kind of exercise they were used to, even with the cold winter months. They were restless, and it didn't settle Dev's nerves any.

"I called in North Star," Cody said once they were all in the barn. "Shay has a bomb expert on her team. He's in Washington right now, so I'll have to go back in there and—"

Pretty much everyone shouted "no" at him before he could finish that idiotic statement.

"He can video chat and instruct on—"

"No."

"You want one of the County guys going in there and getting blown up? You want to wait around for some state official?" Cody demanded, impatience bubbling.

"I want that more than I want you blown to bits," Grandma Pauline said, Nina and Brianna nodding emphatically behind her.

"We need to search the entire building. Make sure there isn't anything here that might be a threat," Dev said in a low voice that only Jamison could hear. Obviously the children knew something was wrong, but he wanted to keep them as in the dark about the danger as he possibly could.

Jamison nodded.

"Is a bad man going to come again?" Brianna asked. "Should we hide?"

Poor Brianna had already lived through danger. Months of terror, really. One of those moments right here in this barn when she and Gigi had hidden from men after Cody.

"No, sweetheart," Nina said, kneeling so she could pull Brianna into a hug. "We're all sticking together this time."

"This could be a way to move us," Sarah whispered to Dev and Jamison, clearly also trying to keep her suspicions from the children. "To get us less protected. It could all be a farce."

Dev nodded. "Could. We're going to check to make sure nothing has been moved. We'll keep the doors closed and the girls occupied until we can get help with the bomb. Just stay put for a few."

She scowled at him, but she did in fact stay put as he moved around the stables. There was nowhere he could go where she couldn't see him, unless he went into the far reaches of one of the stalls, which he only did twice. Jamison and Brady handled the other stalls. They even went into the hayloft and rooted around up there.

But there was no sign of anything amiss. No bombs, no evidence anyone besides him and Duke had been in here.

It didn't sit right. None of this did. He was beginning

to understand Sarah's line of thinking. The notes clearly meant something. The threats that—thankfully—didn't end in any harm were meant more to terrorize than to hurt.

But why?

He'd hoped action would mean something, but they could only react. The only way to act was to figure out what Anth was trying to accomplish, if it wasn't actually sentencing anyone to death.

And why hadn't he gotten a letter? Logically, Dev had kicked this all off by trying to take Ace down all those years ago when Anth had basically saved his life. Saved his life only to take it? That didn't make sense either.

Dev shrugged off his coat and put it on Sarah. How had she ended up one of the people without one?

"I'm not that cold."

"You're not that warm." He turned to the group all crowded in the center of the stables. "I can't find anything out of the ordinary or any evidence someone besides us has been in here."

"What I can't figure is how did he get inside the house? We've had lookouts. We've got everything locked up tight and I didn't notice anything amiss. How could he have been inside to plant the bomb?" Gage asked, cradling Claire to his chest. "How could he have known *I'd* be one of the ones to go get the Christmas decorations?"

"Maybe it was just…coincidence." Felicity looked at the girls and then leaned forward to whisper, "He was going to blow up the house with all of us in it."

"Felicity's right. It didn't have to be you," Dev said, scratching a hand through his hair as he tried to make sense of it. "Isn't that the point? This is all just…theatrics. We're all still alive and well. No one's been hurt—and if he can plant a bomb in the basement, surely he could catch us off guard and hurt us. Sarah was right with the last one. This is some kind of warped game."

"How much longer do we live like this?" Liza demanded.

"We know Brady's note will come next. Soon, if pattern follows. Maybe we can set some kind of trap," Sarah offered hopefully.

"Unless he sends a messenger," Cody pointed out.

"But we'd still have *someone*, if we could catch the messenger. Someone who would have some clue as to what's going on," Dev replied.

"But the notes have come in a variety of ways. How could we possibly predict when and how the next one is going to come?" Brady asked.

"It's not a bad angle. But we know one thing for sure. He's close. Really close. He got in the *house*. We need to know how," Gage insisted.

"Whatever this is, it's planned. Really planned." Dev realized maybe even more than they'd thought. "Ace has been dead for over a year. If that was the tipping point? He's had all that time to plan. And who knows—maybe it wasn't the tipping point. Maybe he's been planning this for a lot longer. I haven't had any interaction with Anth since that day over a decade ago. The ways he could have gotten into the house are legion if we go back farther than we've been on guard."

"So, why now?"

Dev shook his head. "I couldn't say. But, to Sarah's point, it's all planned. It's careful, and even if it's not logical, there's a pattern. It's not random and even if it doesn't make sense to us, there's some thread of sense. If we can access it, we can stop it."

"And if we can't?"

"There's an end game. There has to be. We just have to keep fighting until it gets there." He looked around the stables. His entire family. Everyone he loved. Everyone he…

Sarah's hand slid into his. He looked down at her, pregnant with his child. So determined to figure out the pattern. When he wanted to act, she wanted to sit and think it through—and he figured the opposite was also true.

Balance. They had it—always had. Evened each other out, even when they were bickering. Or were they always bickering because it had been the only way to get him to engage at all for a while there?

She'd brought him back to life, whether he'd wanted to admit that for a very long time or not. It was true. She and the baby were the last missing piece and that was why he was scared of them—better to believe he didn't deserve it than reach for something that might bring him back to fully living.

But there were bigger things to be scared of—real things. Anth and losing any of these people to a madman's whims. He'd once vowed to fight everything

Ace was and touched, but he'd given up on that when he'd almost died.

But there was too much at stake to ignore who and what he was. "There's too much at stake to lose, so we'll figure out a way to win."

Chapter Fourteen

Eventually between the local police department and Cody's connections to the North Star group, a bomb expert was called in. It took most of the day, but they managed to defuse and take away the bomb.

Jamison and Cody had talked about the technicalities. All the Wyatts currently employed by Valiant County helped the other officers dust for prints and try to figure out how Anth, or someone else, had gotten in to plant the bomb.

But there were no answers to be had. Everyone was on considerable edge. The house didn't feel safe. Nowhere felt safe.

Cody and Dev had set out to change all the locks in the house. Brady and Gage had gone out with the other officers to do a sweep of the property. Jamison, Duke and Tucker were keeping a watch on the outdoors with Felicity and Nina, while Rachel, Grandma and Liza were entertaining the girls by decorating the tree.

Sarah was superfluous—in actuality and size. She couldn't do anything fast. She couldn't do *anything*.

She sat on the couch looking at the twinkling lights, feeling sorry for herself and thinking how pointless she was.

Which didn't do anyone any good. Maybe she couldn't *act* in the ways she might like, but she could still think. She *had* to think.

When Cecilia came into the room, she looked... drawn. Sarah wasn't sure what she'd been doing upstairs, but it certainly hadn't been resting up for her night assignment of lookout.

Sarah motioned her to come sit next to her. Cecilia made her way through the Christmas debris, giving Brianna's braid a little tug on the way. Brianna grinned up at Cecilia, then went back to unwrapping ornaments.

Cecilia plopped on the couch next to Sarah and sighed. "Seems so weird to be doing normal things."

"It's almost Christmas," Sarah offered, even though she'd had the same negative reaction this morning.

"Yeah. And we're dealing with bomb threats and hanging up crystal angels."

Cecilia sounded somewhat disgusted, but Sarah had begun to accept it was comforting. Stars and angels and all the symbols of the season of peace on earth and goodwill toward men.

Too bad there was one man she didn't have much peace or goodwill for. Brady would be next, if the notes kept following the pattern. Maybe that was why Cecilia looked so worried. While they were all family and all loved each other, it was probably more stressful when your husband was the next target of unknown sentencing.

Sarah should probably let it be. Focus on Christmas and hope, but… Well, there had to be some way to figure out what was coming next. "Tell me about when you and Brady faced off with Elijah."

Cecilia sighed. "I don't really want to relive that particular moment in my life, Sarah."

"Even if it helped us figure out what's next?"

Cecilia scowled. "I don't see how it would," she grumbled, but she scooted closer to Sarah on the couch so she could speak in low tones the girls wouldn't hear over their chattering. "It all started with me hiding Mak from Elijah." Cecilia's friend had had a baby with Ace's protégé in the Sons. When the mother had been hospitalized, Cecilia had taken the baby to keep him from going to Elijah. She and Brady had worked to keep Mak safe from both Elijah and the dangerous reach of the Sons.

"You miss him."

Cecilia shrugged. "I'm happy Layla's happy. Jarrod is good for her and spending a few weeks with his family in Denver is great for all of them. But, yeah, I miss having them closer."

"So, in reality, you started it."

"Excuse me?"

"I mean, you took Mak and Brady got involved. Before that, Felicity was the one being framed for murder, and Gage got involved. In fact, Felicity was the one who shot Ace, even if he did survive."

"Well, yeah, but—"

Sarah straightened in her seat, trying to find a more comfortable position for her belly. "And Nina went on the run because Ace threatened *her*. She came back because Ace sent men after *her*. Liza came to Jamison when Gigi disappeared."

"What's your point? The only reason the Wyatt boys are ever in trouble is because of us? Sorry, that doesn't fly."

"No, but listen. Why wouldn't you guys be targets too? Why wouldn't he come after Liza, Nina or Felicity? You? Even Rachel was involved because of Duke, which had nothing to do with Ace, even if it did connect to the Sons."

"I don't know." Cecilia's eyebrows drew together. "Well, technically someone shot at Liza."

"Shot *at*, not killed. Regardless, the letter referencing that was to Jamison, not to Liza." Sarah grabbed Cecilia's arm. "What if it's not about Ace?"

"How could it not be about Ace?"

"I don't know." But it made more sense. Liza, Nina and Felicity had had specific run-ins with Ace. Cecilia had been involved with his protégé being hurt. The women should be more involved, but Anth was focused solely on the brothers.

Of course, they were the actual relations to him. Was it about blood? Brotherhood?

"The notes all say treason. I thought it had to do with leaving the Sons, but is it something more? Something…personal? Beyond Ace, I mean."

Cecilia took some time to think that over. "Well, we don't know how Anth was raised. Ace was in the

Sons, but by all accounts Anth wasn't there. Nor was his mother there."

"Our mother." She'd had to explain her blood connection in the barn this afternoon, and she could feel the *pity* from all her sisters. That her parents hadn't been bad people and were now dead. That she was connected by blood to someone terrorizing them.

Cecilia smiled sadly. "I know that's…"

Sarah shrugged. "I don't know what it is. I haven't had time to work it out really." She rubbed her belly, hoping her baby never had to have complicated feelings about their parentage. "But you're right. He wasn't with his parents that we know of. Until after the Wyatts were all out of the Sons."

"It's possible he was there in the few years Liza was out, but it seems unlikely."

"Still, he was with Ace when Dev tried to arrest him. So, wherever he was, he knew Ace. He was working *with* Ace. Even if he did help Dev, he's connected to Ace."

"Maybe the betrayal is a deeper familial sense. Maybe he's not blaming them for Ace, but they didn't come for him. They didn't help him. They all got out, but he… We don't know what he did, but maybe it was terrible."

"But he made Dev promise not to tell anyone about him," Sarah pointed out, though she thought there had to be something to this line of reasoning. Something about family and connections. Not just Ace. It had to be more. Or the brothers wouldn't be singled out the way they were.

Cecilia sighed deeply. "I wish I thought all these mental circles would get us somewhere, but I think we just have to wait. Wait for him to make a mistake and hope…" Cecilia didn't finish her sentence and shook her head.

Sarah got the feeling she was worried about Brady being next to get a letter. About him being the next target. Even though no one had been hurt yet, anyone *could* have been by the bomb. Anyone *could* have been shot. It seemed a bit of blind luck that they were all still intact.

Still, it was disturbing to see Cecilia, of all people, look so…worried and helpless.

"You're a fighter," Sarah said, hoping to see some of Cecilia's usual stubborn surety.

"We're all fighters. But even fighters get tired." Her hands briefly touched her stomach and Sarah's eyes went wide. She wouldn't have thought anything of it if she hadn't spent the past nine months touching her stomach, just like that.

Cecilia's cheeks turned red.

"Are you…"

"I don't know for sure yet," Cecilia hissed, looking around the room to see if anyone was paying attention to them. No one seemed to be. "Don't say *anything*."

Sarah's eyes welled with tears. She couldn't help it. She'd have her son soon, Nina would follow in a few months, and then Cecilia. And they'd all be cousins and…

"Stop that right now," Cecilia said, pointing her

finger in Sarah's face. "We are being *terrorized*. No crying over *potentially* happy things."

"But that's exactly *when* you should cry over such things. Bad doesn't blot out the good, Cee."

"No, no it doesn't." Cecilia took Sarah's hand and gave it a squeeze. "But I'd sure like to be done with the bad."

"We will be." They had to find a way. Not just for her baby, but for *all* their kids. For all of them. For family.

DEV COULDN'T REMEMBER a time he'd been this revved and this exhausted at the same time. Two days had passed without a letter for anyone. No more dead bodies. No more attacks. Just tension and stress and so many questions he didn't have the answer to.

Sarah had floated her theory that whatever was going on had less to do about Ace's death and more about family in general, but Dev still didn't know how to wrap his head around that.

His brothers had never had any interaction with Anth—hadn't even known about his existence. Dev had only interacted with Anth once, and under the promise he'd never let anyone know about him.

Three days of nothing didn't make the obsessing over it any easier. In fact, it made it more frustrating. He couldn't shut off his mind. He could only think. Not one of his favorite places to be—and he couldn't do what he usually did when that happened—bury himself in the ranch.

No, there were people around constantly. He

didn't even get his own room to sleep in what with the crowded house. Every night he went into his own room after Sarah had fallen asleep in his bed and slept on the floor.

But Sarah wasn't asleep tonight like she should be. She was all cuddled up in his bed, but sitting up, leaning against the headboard.

Something heavy shifted in his chest. A dream realized. Except Sarah was *not* his dream. He'd never let himself dream about a future because he'd been adamant there wouldn't be one.

Wasn't that the best way to avoid pain and failure?

But she made all those walls he'd built crumble, and he felt more like he'd been at twenty and stupid than he was now. He knew what could go wrong when you reached for everything. He'd had the scars to prove it.

She smiled at him and he didn't know how he'd survive any of this, even if they caught Anth and everything went back to normal.

"You should be asleep."

She sighed. "I've tried. Brain's too jumbly tonight. I hate that nothing has happened. I keep thinking if I could just work out some missing piece, we'd be able to set a trap for the next note. But if it never comes…"

"It'll come," Dev replied. This wasn't over. That's what Anth's first note had said. Which meant nothing ended until it was *over*.

"I know. That's why I can't stop thinking."

"Yeah, I think we're all having that problem." He

couldn't seem to get himself to move inside the room. Instead he just leaned against the door frame.

"We share a mother. Anth and I. There should be some…bond of connection. Like you have with your brothers."

"We grew up together. It isn't blood that bonded us. It was everything we survived. I don't have any bond with Anth and we share a father. I've actually met him, even if it was only once."

Sarah looked down at her belly, smoothed her hands over the bump. "It's weird…isn't it? There's a connection here, and he's coming at us when I'm nine months pregnant?"

"There's no way he could know that, Sarah. Our own family didn't."

"I know. I just… It's the thinking. He's making us wait on purpose because he has to know we're sitting here driving ourselves crazy trying to understand him. And we can't, can we? We don't know him. I grew up knowing I was adopted, but loved. So loved. I didn't remember anything about my parents, and I'm not saying I never thought about them, but I was given a life I could never resent. I really doubt he had that."

"Yeah. But he wasn't with the Sons, so it was possible."

Sarah shook her head, her blond hair falling out of its messy braid. Her hair on his pillowcase made his heart ache all over again, but she kept talking about Anth and danger, and for the first time in his life he didn't want to focus on the bad.

"He wouldn't have hooked up with Ace, wouldn't

have scared my mother enough to leave me with Duke and Eva, if he had some good life somewhere."

"Maybe."

She fixed him with a look—one of *those* looks that meant she had some...plan or *something*. A battle light, he would call it. He was too weary to figure out an excuse to walk away—get away from Sarah's constant battles.

Or, you kind of like them.

"What was it like to grow up in the Sons?" she asked, clasping her hands over her stomach.

That was not the battle he'd expected, and in hindsight he probably should just walk away. But the answer wasn't as traumatizing as she was probably expecting.

"I don't know." At her sharp look, he shook his head. "It sounds flippant, but it isn't. I don't... It feels like it all happened to someone else. I don't try to remember and the more I don't, the more foggy it gets."

"Did you feel alone?"

He scrubbed a hand over his face. "No. I always had Jamison, and... I think we remember our mother a little better than the younger ones. I think she loved us, but..."

"But what?"

"Her whole life was survival. Her own. We were... pawns of that survival. Which sounds harsher than I mean it. It's hard to blame her...doing what she could to stay alive."

"Couldn't she have escaped back to Grandma Pauline like you all did?"

Dev shrugged. These days he couldn't seem to feel anything for his mother except a sort of pity. What little he remembered of her was of a woman beaten down by...everything. "Maybe. I don't think she knew how. Whatever...whatever attracted her to Ace kept her a victim of his mind games. Or maybe she didn't want to leave. I was a kid. I don't know. I know she feared for her life, but hell, maybe she liked that."

Sarah grimaced, but Dev couldn't deny the possibility. There were too many awful things he'd seen and endured to think some people didn't enjoy or crave that kind of thing.

"After your mother died, what happened?"

"I don't know. We kept...living. Jamison took care of us. Kept us together. Taught us how to survive and planned our escapes. He stepped into her role, I guess. And did a better job of it."

"Anth didn't have either. Not a loving family. Not even the Sons."

"We don't know what he had."

"No. We don't. But what if he had nothing?"

Dev had the uncomfortable memory of what his father had done to them all at seven—except Cody, who they'd managed to get out before Ace's...ritual.

"There's no record of Anth Wyatt," Dev said carefully. "It's possible... Well, what if Ace kept him isolated from everyone? He expected us to be able to survive in the wild at the age of seven. Why not Anth too?"

"What do you mean survive in the wild?"

He cursed himself for forgetting himself. Forgetting that there were things he didn't want to get into. Didn't want to rehash. *Like all of it?*

But it was Sarah, nine months pregnant with his child, who was waiting for an answer. Who was trying to understand, and he didn't have it in him to change the subject. Not when she was in his bed, her hands on her stomach where his own child's heart beat.

"Ace had a ritual. When we turned seven, he'd leave us in the Badlands by ourselves. We had to survive on our own with no supplies for as many days as years we were old every year on our birthdays."

"At *seven*?" Sarah demanded, wrapping her arms protectively over the child inside of her.

That child would never know the kind of terror Dev had known, if he could help it. If he had any say. He'd lay down his own life to keep that child happy and safe. He cleared his throat, hoping to deflect the wave of emotion. "I was twelve when Jamison got me out of there. He had to do it until he was eighteen."

"Jamison being stuck in that awful place longer than you were doesn't mean your trauma wasn't bad. Twelve days all alone in the Badlands when you were a baby."

"I was hardly a baby."

"You were. Seven or twelve or whatever. And it *is* a trauma. It's awful. No kid should have to survive it."

"But… The thing is, Sarah? We did. We survived it and here we all are. Still surviving." Which was a much more hopeful thought than he'd had in a long while.

Survival… He had done that. For years on end—as a kid, then after his coma and injuries. Survival he was good at.

But his brothers hadn't just survived. Now they were all living. Building. Shouldn't he be doing the same? Wasn't it time to build?

No. Right now was still survival. "We should go to bed. Rest while we can. You especially."

She nodded, still studying him with that speculative look. Then she glanced at his sleeping bag on the floor. "You know, you don't have to sleep on the floor. You're certainly not getting much rest."

"Less to do with the floor and more to do with… you know, constant danger."

She pulled back the covers and scooted over in the bed. "There's plenty of room."

All those complicated emotions that had been crashing around inside of him stilled under that very not-innocent offer.

He cleared his throat. "I don't think—"

"Oh, don't be so…*you* about it. I'm just offering to share your bed. It is yours, after all. You deserve a good night's sleep too."

"I'm pretty sure that bed was made for two, not for three."

She rolled her eyes. "Just come to bed."

He should ignore her. Turn off the lights and climb into his sleeping bag. Stick with sanity, reason and just taking time to…evaluate the situation. But when he turned off the light, she turned on her phone, the light a guiding beacon as if he didn't know the way to his bed by heart.

It wasn't really that big of a deal. She was just offering him part of his bed. He'd sleep next to her and nothing would happen. This didn't mean anything. Or didn't have to. It was just a better place to sleep.

Gingerly, he got into his own darn bed.

She laid the covers over him, then curled up next to him—her pregnant belly pressing against his side, her head nudging onto his shoulder until he had to put his arm around her. She laid her hand on his chest and moved in closer.

There was a physical pain in the center of his chest, right where she placed her hand. He didn't know what it was, only that it made it hard to breathe. He felt... everything.

For a man who'd spent a lot of time focusing on feeling nothing, it wasn't just overwhelming, it was paralyzing. But she didn't do anything. She just lay there, snuggled up against him, her hand resting over his raging heart.

Until, second after second, he relaxed. It wasn't going to kill him—probably. Sleeping like this was just...

"It'd be nice, wouldn't it?" she asked, her voice soft and...something else. Something he didn't associate with Sarah. That vulnerability she was trotting out all of the sudden.

"What?" he asked gruffly, wishing he didn't feel so clumsy with her.

"This."

Nice was not the word. That was too easy, and this was…all those things he'd never given himself a chance to believe in. He had his family, but it wasn't…*this*. He didn't have a choice about loving his family, caring about their well-being. He didn't have a choice about being bonded with his brothers over everything they'd been through.

He had a choice with Sarah, because he'd been making the choice to ignore and avoid for years now. There was too much at stake to change his mind, but she kept…changing it anyway.

It's what she'd always done. Pulled him out of or away from his worst impulses. She was always giving to him, and what did he ever give to her?

He'd keep her safe, come hell or high water, but didn't she deserve more than just *safe*? Didn't she deserve the things he'd told himself he didn't. A partnership and…

She cared about him. Enough to fight for him. Didn't she deserve him to care back?

He placed his hand over hers on his chest. "I guess it would."

She chuckled into his neck. "You guess. Such a sweet talker."

"I wasn't *trying* to sweet-talk you."

"No. Why would you need to when I'm throwing myself at you?"

"You're not throwing yourself at me."

Her lips grazed his jaw. "Aren't I?" she asked huskily.

That pain in his chest turned into heat—made all

the hotter by how much he remembered of their night together. It had haunted him all this time, because nothing else had ever stayed with him, moved him, *changed* him quite like that.

Maybe it had taken time to come to grips with the change, but it had started then.

He still held her hand on his chest. She had small hands, but they were rough from ranch work. She was small in general, even with the baby belly, and yet she was one of the strongest, hardest ranchers he'd ever worked beside.

"Sarah…"

"Dev…" she returned, clearly mocking the gravity in his voice.

"I don't know what I have to offer you."

She shifted, her arms sliding around his neck. "It's pretty simple. All I want is you."

Which reminded him of what Jamison had said. *Sometimes being you is enough.* But Dev thought maybe Jamison had it wrong. It wasn't just being yourself—it was wanting to be more of yourself because of someone.

Because of her. Because of Sarah he wanted to be better. To live. To give. It was a terrifying realization, but there was so much terror going on around them, real, psychological terror, that his feelings for her didn't seem quite so overwhelming. Not such a disaster.

No, it seemed a bit like…those good things he'd convinced himself he couldn't have because of a decision he'd made in his early twenties while being beaten almost to death by his father.

Maybe it was time to forgive that kid, just like he would have forgiven all of his brothers—just like his brothers had forgiven him.

Forgiveness seemed too complicated a concept when she was kissing him, pressed up against him, in his bed. He could figure out forgiveness later. For tonight he could just be him. Just be what she wanted. Later he'd worry about being what she needed.

He pulled Sarah's hand from his chest and pressed a kiss to her palm. Then to her wrist. He shifted onto his side and slid her arm up and over his shoulder. Her belly was between them, a reminder that no matter what happened, they'd created life together.

She'd brought him back to life because of it. So he kissed her. He let himself pour all the different emotions inside of him into her—fear and worry and all those dark spaces he didn't think were good enough. These small little buds of life inside of him, of revival. The tiny but growing warmth of hope she'd given him, year after year.

She kissed him back with all of her strength and determination. No surrender or passive acceptance— a challenge, because she'd always been one. And he thought, she always would be one. Which seemed about right. It seemed like just the thing he needed.

But she was soft. There were vulnerable parts to her. It wasn't all strength against strength—her hard head against his. No, they'd have to explore these more tender areas too.

Which right now felt like heaven.

She sighed against his mouth, languid and perfect. "I love you," she murmured.

The words had him freezing.

She didn't stop moving against him. "You don't have to say it back. You don't have to feel it yet. I've got quite the head start."

"I don't…" It was all too much. Every time he thought he was taking this small, positive step—she flipped everything on him.

"And I know you didn't *know* I was in love with you this whole time because I didn't really admit it to myself." She kissed the corner of his mouth, held tight around his neck. "I was talking with Cecilia the other night about everything and… Well, we shouldn't ignore Christmas or love just because someone wants to hurt us."

"No, we shouldn't. Sarah, I—"

"And you're not there yet. It's okay." She pressed her mouth to his. "Don't stop," she murmured against his lips. "Ignore everything I've said."

But how could he ignore *love*? How could he go back to the place he'd been when she'd introduced a whole new level? One he didn't understand.

One she deserved. And if she deserved it, didn't that mean he needed to find it in himself to figure it out? "I don't know where I am. I'm not even sure I know *who* I am. I don't know how to love or how to be a partner. I've been…dormant or something."

"That's ok—"

"Would you let me *talk*?"

"It's just, if you say it now, it's only because of the baby. Because of danger. It wouldn't be real if you said it now."

He understood what she meant, and yet he didn't find himself nodding in agreement. There was a denial inside of him, and that meant all he had was the truth. "I don't understand half of what I feel about you, but it's all real."

She inhaled sharply, but she didn't let him go. She didn't wriggle away. She held him tighter. "Then show me."

Chapter Fifteen

For the first time in her life, Sarah woke up next to a naked man. It was quite an interesting position to be in.

In the early morning light, she could study him. The blanket was only pulled up to his waist, so his entire upper body was bared to her. All the things she hadn't been able to see last night. The impressive lean muscle of his arms from all the work he did. The smattering of dark chest hair.

There were scars. She wanted to trace them, find some way to soothe those old hurts. Those old betrayals.

She'd told him she'd loved him and he hadn't run away. Granted, she'd been throwing herself at him in the moment, but still. He'd stayed. He'd made love to her anyway.

She knew he'd take his time, and he'd make sure that what he felt was love, and that he could give it to her. Which didn't make it hard to wait for an answer, all in all. He'd find those answers. He was just a little on the slow side when it came to emotional stuff.

He'd get there. He wouldn't have slept with her if he didn't think he could get there.

Slept with her. She couldn't help the silly grin that spread across her face. The world around them might be falling apart thanks to their shared half brother, but together she finally had everything she wanted.

And wasn't that the way? Hopes and dreams never seemed to come true conveniently, and danger never seemed to wait for the appropriate moment to make an appearance.

His eyes blinked open. He stared at her and then the room around them. "It's morning."

"Seems to be."

He got up on his elbows, frowning at the door. "No one woke me up for my turn as lookout."

"I mean, or they didn't…want to interrupt."

Dev blinked once, and then a slow horror crept over his expression. She couldn't help it. It made her laugh.

"I'm glad you find it funny," he grumbled, tossing off the covers and getting out of bed.

Sarah watched avidly and with some disappointment as he pulled on boxers, then jeans. He grabbed socks from his dresser and when he sat down to put them on, he did so on her side of the bed.

He looked down at her, still lying on his pillow. She was sure her hair was a tangled mess and she likely looked as haggard as she felt. Still, he reached out and smoothed some hair off her cheek with a gentleness that had a lump forming in her throat.

"You haven't had any contractions?"

Despite the emotion swallowing her whole, she was determined to play this off as no big deal. If she convinced him it was just normal, just *good*, maybe he wouldn't talk himself out of it. "No, your penis did not spur me on to labor."

He rubbed his hands over his face, but he ended up laughing. "You always say the damnedest things."

She grinned at him. "It's part of my charm."

He stared at her so long the grin started to die. It was too serious a look, too serious a study.

"It is," he finally said, with great gravity. "Are we really going to do this? Love each other. Raise this baby together. Be a family. Are you sure that's what you want?"

And there it was. On another man she might call it uncertainty. But she'd been there when he'd survived being beaten near to death by his own father. It was a caution ingrained in him from all the ways life hadn't been fair.

But in that tragic, unfair childhood he'd had Jamison. And Grandma Pauline. So she truly believed…he had the capacity to move past that caution. If given the right push. "I conned you into being the father of my baby, didn't I?"

"I'm serious. I know you set a goal and go after it. I know you accomplish everything you want to. It's who you are and… I admire that about you. But you have to be sure this is really what you want."

She had to take a breath at that, because as much as she loved him, she wasn't so sure he saw her for what she was. Wasn't sure anyone did. She had walls and facades of her own.

But he'd cut to the heart of her. "I imagine there will be some surprises along the way," she said slowly, trying to work through the right words. But sometimes there was no right word, no plan. There was only...honesty and heart. She didn't like those times, but she knew if she was going to get through to Dev on a permanent level, she'd need to offer that to him. "Some hard times. But...we've already done that. I don't know why it would change. Not when we love our ranches, our families. We want to raise this baby together. It's not some fairy tale I've envisioned. It's what we already have. Only together."

His hand was still on her face, still gentle. He seemed to sit and carefully absorb each word. Then he leaned down and pressed a quick kiss to her mouth. "I'm going to go make sure nothing happened last night."

She nodded, but she pulled the covers back. "I'm coming too. But it'll take me about an hour to get there so you go ahead."

He helped her out of bed first, but then he left the room while she got dressed and then headed for the bathroom. She wasn't haven't contractions, but she definitely felt weird this morning. Maybe she just needed to eat.

After pulling her hair back in a sloppy ponytail, she headed for the kitchen. She stopped short at the way a majority of her family was huddled around the table. Felicity and the girls were missing, as were

Duke, Rachel and Tucker—who were probably out doing chores.

"Oh, no. What is it?"

"Brady's letter came," Dev said flatly.

"How?"

"Knives," Brady replied, his voice void of any inflection. Sarah stepped closer and there were a variety of daggers in plastic bags on the table. Along with the letter. She assumed they'd put the knives in the bags in the hope there'd be fingerprints on them—but Sarah doubted it.

"What does it say?"

"'Brady Wyatt,'" Cecilia read before her husband could, acidity dipping from every word. "'Crimes: The subject has been the perpetrator of a wide variety of crimes since childhood. Extreme stalking, harassment, kidnapping, manslaughter and treason. Sentencing: For these acts, I do hereby sentence Brady Wyatt to death. This will be meted out at the judge's discretion through the method B. Wyatt will remember from his father.'"

Sarah turned her gaze to Brady. Clearly he knew what that last line meant, but he made no effort to explain, didn't *want* to explain.

At least, until Cecilia slid her hand over his on the table. Then he let out a long sigh. "It's knives. Ace used to throw them at me. I'm pretty sure the six knives on the door were Ace's." He gestured to the blades on the table. "Like, actually his collection. Passed down to Anth, with the stories of what Ace did to me, I assume."

"Well, you don't go outside, he can't throw knives at you. Problem solved," Cecilia said fiercely.

Brady's mouth curved slightly, as if he was trying to offer Cecilia a reassuring smile and failing.

Rachel, Duke and Gage came inside, snow clinging to their hair. They were still wearing their coats and boots instead of leaving them out in the mudroom. "Another letter?" Duke said gravely.

Brady nodded.

"Take off your gear now and come eat. All of you sit down and eat," Grandma Pauline insisted. She frowned at Rachel's back. "What's on your coat, sweetheart?"

"My coat?"

Grandma Pauline reached out for the back of Rachel's coat, but she stopped short. "Duke."

"What is it?" Rachel demanded.

"Don't move," Duke said sharply. His gaze moved to Tucker, who moved around to Rachel's back too.

Tucker swore, but it wasn't an angry kind of swearing. There was a horrified note to his tone.

"What's going on?" Rachel demanded. She started to reach back, but Tucker took her hand.

"You've got a note pinned to your coat," he said, his voice rough.

"What? That's impossible."

Everyone at the table immediately got up and crowded around Rachel's back. Sure enough, there was a piece of paper safety-pinned to the back of her coat.

Tucker's letter.

Tucker Wyatt
Crimes:
    The subject has been the perpetrator of a wide variety of crimes since childhood. Following in his brother's footsteps, he has committed treason with the terrorist North Star group, along with falsifying evidence, and involvement in false arrest and imprisonment.
Sentencing:
    For these acts, I do hereby sentence Tucker Wyatt to death. This will be meted out at the judge's discretion through the method T. Wyatt deemed acceptable through his own connection to the terrorist group.
    —AW

"He broke the pattern," Sarah said. "He didn't try to hurt Brady first before he delivered Tucker's letter."

"Someone get some gloves and get this off her," Tucker snapped, which was rare for the usually even-keeled Tucker.

Sarah turned to Dev. "What do you think it means? He broke the pattern."

Dev's eyebrows drew together. "Tomorrow is Christmas Eve. He says we all committed treason, and the only betrayal we could have done in his mind would be against the Sons. Family? Ace? Maybe it all...culminates on Christmas?"

Jamison worked to get the safety pin and letter off of Rachel's coat without disrupting any potential fingerprints.

"So where's yours?" Tucker said.

Dev inhaled sharply. Sarah slid her hand into his. She had a terrible feeling about all this—about Dev not getting one first, or with this back-to-back set. About *everything* accelerating beyond the pattern she was still struggling to make sense of.

"I don't know," Dev said, squeezing her hand. "I really don't know."

THAT NIGHT, Dev listened as Jamison outlined all the local police were doing, and how the feds were getting involved.

"No prints on anything. The bomb was dangerous. It could have done some significant damage and they've sent it on to the feds to see if they can track down who bought the materials. But as for evidence we'll be able to use against him? Nothing."

Dev didn't feel in any way, shape or form comforted. Nor did any of his brothers.

The letter on Rachel's coat was the biggest concern. Had he been in the mudroom and put it on the coat? It seemed unlikely that hadn't been noticed until after they'd come in for chores. But how had Anth, or whomever, gotten close enough to pin it on to Rach's coat without her knowing?

"It's impossible. Both scenarios are impossible. She wasn't alone for no one to notice and someone *would* have noticed beforehand." Tucker stalked the kitchen. His normal calm demeanor even in crisis was gone—probably since the note had been pinned to his fiancée's actual person.

Sarah was the only woman in the kitchen. Cecilia had taken Rachel upstairs under the guise of wrapping presents—but what Dev was sure was an effort to take her mind off the fact that Anth had possibly been close enough to touch.

Liza and Nina were giving the girls baths, and Grandma Pauline was doing laundry while Felicity and Duke were in the living room encouraging Claire to walk.

Life went on, even as it was threatened.

"They'll run the prints on the knives, the new letters, and look for any kind of DNA on Rachel's coat, but hard to believe he'd leave anything," Jamison continued. "And we're using up a lot of the county's resources while not being able to fully work."

Tucker swore under his breath. All his brothers looked grim. Dev glanced at Sarah. She was standing there, worry lines etched across her face as she rubbed her stomach.

She'd been the one to focus on the pattern. The idea it wasn't as cut and dried about Ace as they might think. She was the one to put the idea in his head.

This was about *him*. His brothers might be getting the notes and threats—but the absence of him getting one *meant* something.

Dev had the horrible hope it meant he could do something about this. But he'd have to face Anth alone, and he knew no one in his family would go for that.

There was the option to sneak out, but Dev figured that caused more problems than it could solve. He needed his brothers on his side, and he…didn't know how on Earth he'd convince them to let him handle it.

But convincing them in smaller groups was his only chance. He looked around the table, then up at Sarah, who was standing at his shoulder. He wished he could get rid of her, but she'd never leave. She'd assume they were going to make plans without the women, and she wouldn't budge.

So he somehow had to win Sarah *and* his brothers to his way of thinking.

Good luck.

"I think I should go out and do the evening chores on my own." Because he was no orator or persuasive speaker. There was only what he thought and what should be done.

"Right," Cody said sarcastically. "Hop on out there. We'll just huddle up in here and see what happens."

"Well, why not?"

"Because it's idiotic," Sarah said, crossing her arms over her chest. "Possibly the stupidest thing I have ever, *ever* heard you say."

"I have to agree," Jamison said.

"He didn't leave me a note. That means something."

"Maybe you'll get one tomorrow. We don't know what he's doing." Gage shook his head. "Patterns or not, we don't know how to predict what a psycho is going to do. I don't think giving him an easy target is in anyone's best interest."

Dev wasn't so sure. A target was…action. It was

something. It could spur action and that could spur re-action. He could tell he wasn't going to get anywhere with them, though. Too many noble souls, and Dev found he didn't want any of them to sacrifice that.

So, he'd have to figure out another way.

"All right. I'll have Duke go with me." Maybe one-on-one outside he could convince Duke to let him go off on his own. His family would be pissed, but some-one would know where he was.

Dev stood and headed for the living room, but Sarah followed, stopping him in the hallway by grab-bing his arm. "I know that look. That's *my* look."

"What look?"

"A goal. A plan. One you don't want anyone to know about. Grim determination to do things your way, no matter the cost."

He looked down at her and sighed. "I just said I'd get Duke. No going outside alone, so I'm getting your father—you know, the other rancher in this house."

"Aside from me."

"You're out of commission for the time being, Sarah. You know that. Now, the evening chores need to be done with what little daylight we have left."

Still she didn't let go of his arm. "Don't do any-thing stupid. Promise me."

He looked at her and hated how much worry was there. How valid it was. "I don't have a death wish."

"Anymore."

He smiled a little, if only because it was fair enough. "Anymore," he agreed. "It has to end, and

I'm the one… I don't have a letter. I should have been first."

"He warned you. You got an 'it's not over' letter."

"I should have been first. I wasn't. We got two sentencing letters in one morning—and one wasn't for me. I'm the only one who's met Anth. Who even knew he existed. You're the one who said there's a pattern that has to mean something."

"So what if it does?"

"Sarah. At some point, this has to end."

"That doesn't mean you'll be the one to end it alone. We have to end it together." She gave his arm a shake as if to get through to him. "So, promise me."

He didn't know how to promise her something so nebulous. Especially when she didn't mean don't do something stupid, she meant don't get hurt. He couldn't promise that.

"I love you," he said instead, because there was a very good possibility of getting hurt, and she deserved the words. "And I love our baby. I absolutely want to be around. I'm not going to run off half-cocked because I'll let my guilt force my hand."

"But?" she demanded, tears heartbreakingly filling her eyes.

"But, I'll do whatever it takes to protect my family. I *have* to." He placed his hand over her stomach. Any day now, that baby would be born. Any day now, he would have a child in his arms. His own. "I'll do everything I can to survive, but survival means nothing if we don't win."

"It's not about winning."

"Maybe *win* is the wrong word. I don't know what the right one is. I want you all safe. I want this over. I want a *life*. We all deserve one. If I'm the target or the center or the purpose, I can't wait around for *him* to decide how to end it. You're going to have this baby any day now. We need this danger taken care of. Now."

She blinked up at him, a tear falling over on her cheek. It tore him in two. Even if she'd been a little more emotional since she'd gotten pregnant, it didn't ease the pain of seeing her cry. Of knowing *he* was making her cry.

He wiped away the tear for her and she sniffled. She shook her hair back and glared up at him. "If anything happens to you, I'll kill you myself," she said, and then stalked away from him down the hall.

Dev blew out a breath. He wished he could be swayed by her emotions or her threats, but in the end he'd do what he had to do.

Chapter Sixteen

It turned out Sarah didn't have to kill Dev. Yet. He and Duke returned from the evening chores without incident—though Sarah didn't trust the look they gave each other as they came inside.

Sarah let everyone bustle her off to bed. She didn't sleep, but she lay there, eyes open. When the contractions tightened her belly, she watched the time. They were sporadic, and as long as they were, there was no way she was telling anyone about them.

Not while Dev was so determined he had to be the one to solve this horrible problem. No, she couldn't leave him.

He came in halfway through the night after his turn as lookout and slid into bed with her.

"Nothing going on," he murmured as she snuggled into him.

"Good."

"Sleep."

She didn't. It was too hard with the worry on her mind and the contractions popping up without warning. She couldn't be shipped off to the hospital. It was terrible timing. Baby would just have to stay put. Besides, he wasn't due for another day.

She'd power through. She'd read tons of stories about women who'd had long, elaborate labors. Who'd had contractions for days and days before going to the hospital. She would be fine. Especially for her first time, she was certain her actual delivery was a ways off.

It had to be.

Christmas Eve dawned, pearly and snowy. Sarah gave half a thought to how bad the roads would be to get her to the hospital. But it wasn't like a whiteout blizzard or anything. It was just a slow-falling snow that kept accumulating.

She wasn't going to be dumb. She'd tell everyone with more time than she needed. Maybe when her contractions were ten minutes apart. Or if her water broke. That would be her guide.

As the day wore on, lookouts and chores interspersed with Christmas crafts and baking with the girls, she was certain she was right. She could go an hour without having a contraction. Although then they usually sped up for a while after one of those hours before tapering off again.

But they did keep tapering. They weren't regular exactly. And no one noticed. As long as no one noticed they couldn't be *that* bad.

She was pretty sure Dev and Duke had something up their sleeve every time they went to take care of ranch chores, but they always came back. No sign of anything. Except that *look* they gave each other.

Sarah lumbered into the living room after dinner. She'd tried to go to sleep early but she was antsy and uncomfortable.

All her sisters, except Cecilia, were wrapping the girls' presents from Santa. Cecilia was stationed outside the sleeping children's room as lookout.

All the men decided to do a sweep of the property while the women prepared Santa's arrival. Which left Sarah feeling even more antsy. "He's going to do something stupid. I can feel it."

Her sisters and Grandma Pauline looked at her with no small amount of pity.

"I assume you mean Dev," Rachel offered, expertly taping off another corner of shiny red wrapping paper.

"Yes, I mean Dev." Sarah winced as a contraction started—but the doctor had said as long as she could speak through them, she was fine. *Fine.* "One of these times he's not going to come back because..." She had to stop and take a breath—but that wasn't the same as not being able to speak through them. *Right?* "He's off doing something stupid trying to end this all by himself."

"I'm sorry, girl, but stopping a Wyatt boy from doing something stupid is like stopping the Earth from spinning," Grandma Pauline said, curling ribbon with a pair of scissors. Then she looked up at where Sarah was standing, one hand pressing on her belly, desperately trying to arrange her face in something other than a grimace of pain.

"Are you having contractions?" Grandma Pauline demanded.

"Not…really."

"Not *really*?" Liza shrieked, leaping to her feet.

"Just here and there. Very far apart."

"Lord almighty," Grandma Pauline said as all the women started to get to their feet.

"Wait. Where are you going?"

"You have to get to the hospital."

"I can't! We can't. It's not time. You're not supposed to go until the contractions are closer together. Besides, Santa has to come. You have to finish."

"Your contractions might be close together by the time we brave the roads to get to town," Liza said, helping Grandma Pauline to her feet. "Don't be stubborn, Sarah."

"It is not time yet," Sarah repeated, ready to fight them off. She wasn't going anywhere. Not on Christmas Eve. Not with Dev out…doing whatever he was about to do that she was just certain was going to get him hurt.

"Sarah." Grandma Pauline's voice was gentle, which had tears welling in Sarah's eyes. "I know you're scared. That's all right. But we need to go."

Sarah wanted to argue more, but Grandma being gentle with her made her feel…small. Silly. Like maybe all this fixation on Dev doing something stupid was just an attempt to take her mind off the fact that she was in labor. When she didn't know how on earth she was going to push a baby out of her.

Before Sarah could say anything, acquiesce or argue more—because she really didn't know which to do—the door to the kitchen slammed open and footsteps thundered toward them.

"Fire." Tucker stumbled in, panting. "Stables are on fire. Called 911, but—"

Sarah looked around at the women in the room. She could see her sisters were reluctant to go because of her. But the stables weren't just housing the horses for the Reaves ranch right now. They had all the Knight horses too.

She couldn't stand the thought of anything but everyone working to get them safe. "Go. Please. Take care of this first. I promise you, there's time on my end."

Felicity and Nina exchanged a look, Sarah supposed because they'd both given birth. Felicity gave a little nod. But they didn't rush out of the room. "We have to think this could be a trap."

"The horses are in the stables," Sarah said desperately. "And the hoses will be frozen. It'll take forever for the fire department to get out here. If you let the men take care of it, they'll do something extra stupid."

"That's true," Nina agreed, but she looked at Sarah's stomach with some trepidation.

"Nina, stay here and watch the girls with Cecilia," Liza ordered, already heading for the door. "Grandma Pauline, you're on Sarah duty. You'll have Cee and Nina if things get hairy on the labor front."

"I don't need—"

But Liza, Rachel and Felicity were already gone, following Tucker out into the kitchen, which would lead them back outside. There wasn't time to talk it over. Time was of the essence.

Grandma Pauline looked at Nina. "Grab a gun and go guard the girls' rooms with Cecilia. Sarah and I will get the rifles and sit tight on this level."

Rifles. Sarah pressed a hand to her tightening stomach. "He isn't after us. He's after the boys."

Grandma Pauline sighed. "That doesn't mean he won't come after us to get to them."

DEV DIDN'T THINK anyone was under the assumption the fire was just a fire. Jamison had instructed everyone to stay with a partner—one to be part of the bucket brigade, and one to stay close to watch out for any attacks.

Because no one could argue with the fact they had to get the horses out of the stables before the fire consumed them.

There was no way to get hoses working in the sub-zero temperatures, so they'd had to start a bucket brigade, passing buckets of water from the one spigot that wasn't frozen. They'd never be able to put out the fire in its entirety. They just needed a space to get the horses out.

He could hear their worried whinnies, but it looked like the fire had started from the outside. If that was the case, he could still save them.

Jamison was stationed closest to the blaze, determining where to throw the buckets of water.

"I've got to go in," Dev said over the sounds of the howling wind and the crackling blaze. Snow was falling but not at a rapid enough pace to extinguish the man-made fire. The smell of gasoline was almost overwhelming.

It had been set. To get them out here, but the women in the house were armed. Capable of fending off an attack. Every group of people was taking precautions. Though Dev didn't think Anth was going for the house. No, he wanted him out here. Outside where there was less protection, less cohesiveness.

They'd been drawn out to be targets. Dev was sure of that. Once he saved his horses, he'd be whatever target Anth wanted. It was time to end this.

"It's still too dangerous," Jamison said.

Dev shook his head. "Too much longer and we lose the horses. Just water down my coat. It'll only take me a few minutes to get them out."

"It'll take longer than that. You know it will. Those horses will freeze. You're going to have to pull them out. It'll take time."

"Give me three minutes. Just three."

Jamison paused. He took the bucket handed to him. "Your leg?"

"It'll hold up," Dev insisted. He had to save at least some of the horses. They were as innocent in all this as his family was.

Jamison looked down at the bucket he was holding. "All right. This should douse you. You take more than those three minutes…" He trailed off.

"I promise. Dump it on me."

Dev braced himself for the cold, but there was no

fully bracing for the icy cold seeping through his coat. Immediately his teeth began to chatter.

"Three minutes," Jamison repeated.

"Three minutes," Dev agreed. He crouched low, kept his wet sleeve over his mouth, and then moved. The flames had definitely come from the outside, so while the inside was full of smoke, there were only a few places the flames had broken through.

It would only take a few more places of breakage to have the whole place engulfed what with all the straw and hay as tinder. Dev didn't spend any time deliberating. He moved through from one side to the other, opening stall doors.

Like Jamison had predicted, the horses only bucked and neighed in fear of the smoke and flames. It would take more than the three minutes—so Dev set out to do the most he could in what time he had.

He managed to get three out by covering their eyes with rags and leading them with a heavy hand. But after the third, Jamison grabbed him before he could go back in.

"I've got four more to go," he rasped. "I'll go in on the other side. It'll be quick."

"Take Du—"

But Dev broke Jamison's grasp and ran. He couldn't wait for backup or a lookout. He had dwindling time to get his horses safe. He ran to the back of the stables, which was closer to the remainder of the horses. Fire engulfed the frame of the door, but with his wet sleeve covering his arm, he slid the bar out of the way and shoved the door far enough open that he could get the horses out. Then Dev ran inside, keeping low, keeping his mouth covered.

His eyes stung, his throat burned, but he worked to get the four horses out. The last one was the hardest, Sarah's stubborn mare of course being the most difficult.

Dev was about to admit defeat so he didn't die of smoke inhalation, but the horse finally moved forward and then ran off into the dark night.

Dev stumbled to his knees outside the stable, gulping in the fresh air. His throat felt raw, like it had been burned itself. His leg ached in all the normal places but with a piercing pain he hadn't felt in a while. But the horses were safe, even if they were now running all over creation.

Dev looked up to the the the man who stood there waiting for him. It wasn't Duke or one of his brothers. Or at least, one of his full brothers.

"Merry Christmas, brother."

Dev shivered inside his wet coat as he sat back on the snow. He breathed heavily—cold and hot at the same time. Pain in his leg, in his eyes, in his throat. But this was what he'd wanted. A one-on-one. Face-to-face with the man who'd clearly made *him* a target even if he'd used his brothers too as smoke and mirror distractions. "I've been waiting for you, Anth."

Dev couldn't make out much of his features in only the light from the blaze of the fire. The orange glow made him look like some kind of demon from a children's fairy tale.

"Have you now? Seems like you've been conspiring with the brothers who've done so much wrong. Betrayed you and yours over and over again. It doesn't seem like my notes got through to you at all." He held up something in the flickering light, but Dev didn't know what it was.

But something exploded in the distance, a light flashing past the rise. The Knight house maybe, or their stables. Dev couldn't be sure. But he saw as his brothers and sisters-in-law began to run for it.

"That should keep them busy," Anth said cheerfully.

But what Dev hoped to God Anth didn't see was that while a majority of the figures had run off toward the other explosion, it wasn't all of them. Unless they were obscured by the dark, only seven ran for the explosion. That meant at least two were either still on the other side of the barn or running for the house.

Anth laughed as the stables began to moan and creak under the weight of the flames. "You think you know what I want, Dev. But you don't have a clue."

Chapter Seventeen

The contractions were no longer slowing down. Grandma Pauline held her hand while Sarah lay down on the couch and tried not to panic. She couldn't panic about labor when there was a fire and a madman out there.

"Breathe," Grandma Pauline ordered.

Sarah tried to listen, tried to focus on the Christmas lights twinkling around them, instead of her own body. But her thoughts kept whirling around. All the ways this was the worst timing *ever*, and how was she going to make it?

"I was stupid and selfish," she muttered. If she'd told Dev or anyone about her contractions she might be on her way to the hospital, with Dev at her side, rather than worried about him out there fighting fires and trying to save their horses.

"You are young and maybe a little foolish, but neither stupid nor selfish," Grandma said matter-of-factly. "My mother had me in this very house. We both lived to tell the tale. If there wasn't a fire and someone out there likely threatening us, you'd be on your way to the hospital. As it is, we've got a fire truck and an ambulance on the way."

"If they can get here." The 911 dispatchers had been apologetic, but had emphasized how long the response time might be due to weather and available emergency vehicles.

Still, help was coming. Even if she ended up having the baby here, help was on its way. For all of them.

She knew without a shadow of a doubt Anth was out there. Why would there be a fire if he wasn't? And if he was out there, he wouldn't be alone. He'd have backup. Wouldn't he? Enough to outnumber all of them?

Especially while they were busy trying to save her horses. Dev's horses.

"Breathe, Sarah," Grandma Pauline said sternly.

"He's out there. He has to be out there and they're all…"

"Smart individuals who'll do what they can to keep their loved ones safe. We have extra help on the way. You need to focus on you. Your contractions are getting closer and closer together. Let's focus on this little Christmas baby."

Sarah tried to nod. Regardless of what terror might befall them, she was in labor. Actual going-to-have-a-baby-in-a-house labor. No amount of danger, not even an act of God, was going to change or stop that.

"Did your mom have a doctor with her?" Sarah asked, trying to focus on baby-having and baby-having alone. Her son. She had to bring him into the world. Somehow.

"No, ma'am. It was February. A raging storm. Whiteout blizzard, or so she always told. She had my grandmothers with her and that was it. And look at me. Eighty years later, still kicking."

Sarah wanted to smile but another contraction washed over her. She tried to picture it. Eighty years ago. Having a baby with only a mother's guidance in the middle of a blizzard, knowing if something went wrong, that was it. For both of them.

She had help coming. An ambulance for her, fire department for the horses. But where was the police officer who was supposed to have been watching the road? She opened her mouth to say something about him, but there was a commotion in the kitchen and Brady and Liza burst into the living room.

"He blew something up over toward the Knight property," Brady said, coming to kneel next to Grandma Pauline. "Most ran over there, but Liza told me about Sarah. I thought I should be here."

"You got any of your EMT stuff?" Grandma demanded.

"I'll go get it in a second. First, I want to check her out. What are the contractions like?"

"Painful. You're not going to deliver my baby, Brady. That's weird."

He didn't even acknowledge she'd spoken. "How far apart are they?"

"Five minutes," Grandma Pauline said. "On the regular. Imagine it'll get closer and quick."

"Has your water broken?"

Sarah shook her head. "That's good, right? It's still

going to take a long time if my water hasn't broken. Right? You don't have to deliver my baby. It'll be fine. Have you even delivered a baby before?"

Brady offered what she supposed was meant to be a reassuring smile. "It's definitely not a bad sign. As is the fact you're lucid. I'll go get my kit. It won't help with labor per se, but we can get a blood pressure reading and start sterilizing." Brady got to his feet.

"Wait, you didn't answer my question."

But Grandma Pauline waved him on. "Liza, you go with him. Then if the coast is clear you tell everyone fighting those fires to come home. The horses are safe—let the rest burn. Get all those boys inside. Now. If he's out there lurking about, we all need to be together. Things and even houses can be replaced. People can't." Grandma gave Brady and Liza a stern stare. "Now."

Sarah struggled to sit up. "I should help. I should—"

"Sorry. Your one and only job is labor," Brady offered. "You sit tight. Let us handle things." He and Liza rushed out the way they'd rushed in.

"He's out there. He has to be out there." Sarah sagged back onto the couch. She was going to hyperventilate if she didn't calm down. She focused on her breathing. "Anth is out there. He could pick them off. He could—"

"There's all sorts of things he could," Grandma Pauline agreed. "There's also all sorts of things your family can do to thwart him. We'll have Liza bring them all back home, and Brady will get what he can to help you have a safe delivery. We're survivors, Sarah Knight. Don't you forget that."

Sarah swallowed and tried to nod, keeping her hand in Grandma's. Survivors. Yes. All of them were. Fighters, like she'd told Cecilia the other night. Things might be scary, they might look grim, but they'd all faced those things before.

And won. Survived. Lived and continued to love.

Yes, it would be okay. It would have to be okay. Even if everything burned. Even if Brady had to be the one to deliver her baby. They would survive. All of them.

With a pop, the lights went out. Grandma Pauline's hand squeezed hers. "It's all right, girl," she whispered.

But Brady hadn't returned and Sarah knew it definitely was not all right.

Especially when she felt the warm, wet trickle of her water breaking.

"So, WHAT IS IT you want?" Dev managed to ask, though his teeth were chattering so hard it was a wonder he got any words out.

"We have an opportunity. You and me. The chance to do what Ace never could." Anth spoke in much the same way Dev remembered Ace speaking. With a calm, determined fervor. If you didn't know better, it was easy to get swept away in.

Too bad Dev knew much, much better. "L-live normal, s-sane lives?"

Anth snorted. "No. That ship sailed. That's the

kind of thing my mother tried to give me." He scoffed. "Who wants normal? She tried to convince me to settle for so much less than I deserve. I had to hurt her. I had to show her. I was born for so much more. So were you, Dev."

For someone who wanted to do what Ace never could, he sure sounded a lot like their father. Still, Dev couldn't make sense of being singled out. "Why me?"

"Well, for starters, you realized being beholden to law and order was beneath you."

Dev opened his mouth to argue with Anth. His law enforcement career had ended because of the physical limitations of his body, thanks to Ace. But one thing Dev had learned in dealing with Ace: don't try to reason with an insane person.

If he played along he could see what Anth might divulge. If Anth was here, he was far away from the family. If Dev could keep Anth right here, they weren't just safe, they had a chance to end this.

"I had hoped showing you what monsters your brothers were would change the tide, but you remained stubborn about it. You continued to protect them. You saw their crimes. Always protecting them, and for what?"

Dev wasn't sure how to answer. Anth was no more sane than Ace had been. It was almost exactly like talking to his father. He'd feel more sympathy for Anth if he hadn't talked about being made for more than his mother wanted to give him.

In Dev's experience, when someone tried to give

you the escape hatch, you took it. You were grateful for them. Dev hadn't been grateful enough for Grandma and Jamison—dousing too much of it in self-loathing.

But he'd wanted them. Always what they could give, even when he didn't believe he deserved it.

He knew better now. That part of his life was over. He had to find a way to end this with Anth—once and for all.

"Well, y-you c-certainly b-beat us. Though we're still alive, so I'm not sure what the point of those s-sentences was."

"I couldn't kill them," Anth said, as if that was obvious. "That would have turned you against me. Eventually, they'll have to get what's coming to them, but we'll make that decision together. We'll do it together. You do see how wrong they were. How many horrible things they've done. Don't you?"

"Yeah. I mean, I didn't at first." Dev tried to think of what Anth would want to hear. "But your notes were…convincing. I was just confused since you didn't kill them."

"We can. We will. Together. That's what I have to offer you, Devin. A partnership. Building the thing Ace never could. True freedom. True power."

Dev racked his brain for something to say. Some way to agree with Anth, but this was so insane he didn't know how to even pretend to be that out of touch. He tried to think back to his childhood, those fuzzy memories he'd tried to push so far away they never surfaced.

When Ace had raged, what had Jamison done? Played the part. Puffed him up. Made the conversation about Ace, not one of his disappointments or escaped sons.

Dev wrapped his arms around himself, rubbing his hands up and down his coat sleeves, trying to create some warmth. "Y-you've certainly shown you're as s-smart as he was. Smarter," Dev quickly amended.

"It's amazing how easy it is to set traps when you plan for years. Ace taught me that, but I took it farther. I always took what he taught me farther. He could never get the cops on his side. Me? I befriend one underpaid cop, tell him what he wants to hear for *years*, then it's easy to get him to look the other way with a simple down payment."

Dev's stomach curdled. He'd certainly considered the fact Anth had had time to plan. And in that planning had been able to do things like plant the bomb and pin a note to Rachel's coat without them knowing how. Palming a key at some point when they weren't as diligent, knowing their patterns and where one could hide to be close but no one knew.

But paying off a cop—one who worked *with* his brothers—to look the other way. Dev hadn't even considered that once.

"Now things are about to start really going down. So let's cut to the chase. I'm giving you the chance, Dev. To see the error of your brothers' ways. I'm the true brother. I saved your life. And you're a true brother, because you didn't tell them about me. You passed the test. Now it's time to start over. I got rid of Ace—"

"Y-you… Ace died in prison."

"You don't think I arranged that? You don't think I arranged *all* of it. Convinced Ace to go after your brothers. Encouraged him to swim in that psychosis. Ace was flawed. Too obsessed with himself, with you all." Anth sneered. "He cared more about size and numbers and being a *god* than actually acting out his vengeance. He didn't understand that the weak had to be eradicated. The disloyal had to be cut out, root and all. I learned. He kept me isolated. Alone. And I learned the power in being small."

"There's power in family too. In working together. Isn't that what you're proposing? Us? Family?"

"It has to be the right family. Your brothers failed the tests, Devin. They care more about law and order and themselves. But you. You care about the right things. That's why we have to start over. Stay small. Just you and me. You can thank me now, Dev."

Dev tried to work through all that, but decided in the end to just push it away. To just go along with whatever Anth said until they were close enough he could knock that gun out of his hands.

"Thanks," Dev managed, though admittedly it didn't sound very sincere.

"Do you understand what I've showed you? Do you understand what we can build? Not the Sons of the Badlands. We aren't sons. We're power. And power over many corrupts. Ace should have kept us small. He should have focused on family alone. Instead he had delusions of grandeur. We won't do that. Our kingdom will be small, but it will be mighty. And it will be built on our blood alone."

"Our?"

"You're righteous, Devin. Or at least, you have the potential. To keep our bloodline pure. To keep our group strong. We have to start all over. It's taken me years to disband the Sons, to undermine their power and influence. Kind of funny how North Star helped me do that."

Dev's vision was dimming. It was too cold and he was wet. He'd inhaled a lot of smoke despite his best efforts. But he had to stay awake. Stay alive. He couldn't let the elements take him any more than he could let Anth win.

"Now, we'll take over the power vacuum and truly succeed. If you can prove your loyalty. These past few weeks have made me wonder. You've stood by your brothers. Will you stand by me instead?"

"I kept your secret. You're right about that. But I have a quiet life here." Dev tried to think of what words would get through to Anth, but he didn't think there were any. No combination of truth or lies. He couldn't outtalk someone who thought the way Anth did.

"You were made for more, Devin. I think deep down you know that. Don't you know that? Ace was left to die. Through his miraculous—"

"Spare m-me Ace's origin s-story," Dev grumbled. He started to move, in the hopes he could stand. But the gun in Anth's hand went from pointing at the ground to pointing at Dev's heart.

"His origin story is ours. He failed. But we? We can succeed. Based on his foundation. Better. I know he tested the six of you like he tested me. We were made in his image, but better. We can be better, Dev."

"I'm going to stand up or I'm going to pass out and freeze to death right here."

Anth *tsk*ed. "No, I don't think so. Stay seated." He seemed to test the aim of the gun, holding it one way and then another, but always pointed at Dev. "How about this? A test. You pass, you can stand and move on to the next step. You fail? Well…"

Dev didn't think that'd end too well for him, but what other choice was there? If he could stand up, he could lunge for Anth. He could maybe get the gun. Sitting here in the snow he couldn't do a damn thing. "All right."

"Who's the father of Sarah's baby?"

Anth didn't shoot, but the pain that cracked through Dev felt like a shot. "What do you care about that for?" he rasped.

"It's a test, Devin. All you have to do is tell me the truth."

It was impossible to tell what Anth knew. What he didn't. Did he care about Sarah's pregnancy because he knew the baby was Dev's? Even if he'd had Ace killed, even if he viewed Ace with contempt, clearly he was Ace's son—warped in all the ways Ace had been.

The more terrifying thought was he cared because

Anth knew he was related to Sarah. Dev couldn't give this imbalanced psychopath the truth. But a lie might get Dev killed.

"Pretty simple question, Dev. The truth. Or your life."

"I told everyone I was the father, yes." If Anth had been watching them, paying attention, he might know that. He clearly knew *something*, didn't he?

But he couldn't really know that Dev and Sarah had slept together nine months ago. There was no way he'd been at Cecilia and Brady's wedding and actually seen it.

"But?"

Dev took a shaky breath, hugging himself against the bitter cold. "But it isn't true. I'm not the father."

"You just decided to pretend to be?"

Dev couldn't tell if Anth sounded skeptical or interested, so he just...talked. Spewed whatever he could think of to say. "She needed a partner. Someone to help her out. I care about her, so I stepped up." God, he hoped admitting he cared about Sarah didn't make her more of a target. If he could convince Anth of this, he could get Anth away. Promise to join whatever insane group Anth had made up. Pretend to care about some cult.

Whatever it took to get Anth far away from here.

Anth sighed heavily. Then he raised his gun. "You fail the test, Dev. I know you're the father. You don't think I was at Brady and Cecilia's wedding? Watching. Waiting. Figuring. See, that's the difference between Ace and me. He was patient enough for revenge, but he wasn't smart enough to make it matter. To build something from revenge."

Dev fought a wave of nausea—whether from the fire and possible hypothermia or the fact Anth had *been* there. Watching. On what should have been Brady and Cecilia's day with nothing of Ace's to touch them.

But it had touched them all.

"It's a shame you couldn't be honest, because I can't abide liars in our new beginning. But you're not my only chance here. You're not the only one with my blood." Without warning, he pulled the trigger, the bullet hitting Dev with a blast of fire and pain in his gut.

He fell to the ground on a howl of pain. It waved over him, black and all encompassing, but he couldn't let it win. He had to keep Sarah safe.

But Anth had already begun to walk away. Toward the house. Toward Sarah. "Sarah and I will build our kingdom," he said, loud enough to echo through the dark night around them.

"She'll kill you first," Dev managed to grind out, but Anth was already too far away. Whistling as he strode for the house.

Chapter Eighteen

Sarah heard whistling and in that moment she was more terrified than she'd been this whole time. She'd face labor with *no* help if someone wasn't out there... whistling.

"Grandma—"

"Shh."

Sarah felt something being pressed into her hand. The handle of the rifle Grandma had gotten when everyone had run out to fight the fire.

"Hide it," she whispered. Then she let go of Sarah's other hand. Sarah couldn't see, but she could hear the sound of Grandma Pauline getting to her feet. "I've got a flashlight right over there in the curio cabinet. You sit tight."

Sarah didn't want to sit tight. She didn't want to let Grandma Pauline go, and she damn sure didn't want someone to be *whistling* somewhere in the house. And what about Nina and Cecilia upstairs? Would they sit tight? Protect the girls?

Please. Please, stay up there.

The whistling grew closer and closer, and the room

stayed utterly dark. Sarah thought she heard the sound of a drawer being pulled open, but still no flashlight light came on.

The whistling stopped and Sarah held her breath, finger curling around the trigger of the gun even though she had it hidden under the blanket she was lying under.

Then she heard a crack, followed by the sickening thump of a body hitting the floor.

"Stupid old woman. I hope that killed her."

Terror froze her completely still for far too long. She wanted to scream, but her breath was frozen along with the rest of her. Until her body betrayed her with a violent contraction. She groaned and thrashed against the pain, tears leaking out of her eyes. Grandma Pauline.

"*Hope* that killed her" didn't mean she was dead yet, though.

She heard footsteps above.

"Just a warning," the man's voice yelled loudly enough to be heard upstairs. "If anyone comes down those steps, I'll shoot them."

A light switched on, blinding Sarah and causing her to closer her eyes and flinch away.

"What's this? The baby is coming right now? Well, that does mess with my plans. I'll have to think about that," the man's voice said.

Sarah slowly opened her eyes against the steady beam of light coming from a flashlight pointed way too close to her face. She couldn't make out the man holding it. "Where are Brady and Liza?" she managed to rasp. He hadn't killed Grandma Pauline, though he likely had a gun. Maybe he'd missed them too.

But Brady hadn't come back.

"Those two. Who cares about them?"

"I do. *I* do." Tears leaked out of her eyes, but she tried to blink them away. Tried to focus. She had to focus on surviving this.

"Well, it's none of your business, but I haven't killed anyone tonight. Yet. Well, maybe."

"I heard gunshots. I heard…" Maybe. Oh *God*.

"Morons shot at me in the pitch black. I could have been any one of their loved ones. With all that haphazard shooting it was easy enough to turn course and come up behind them. A few quick blows to the head, and some rope, and they won't be a problem for us for a while. Do you know how well I can see in the dark? It's something of a talent I developed. You see, your mother tried to secret you away. Tried to give you light. But I was given nothing but darkness. Isolation in a little shed. I learned to do what needed to be done. To do what Ace could never do."

So he knew. Knew they shared a mother. Knew… everything. "Grandma Pauline. You—"

"Just knocked her in the head too. I didn't *kill* her. If she dies it's her own fault. I need you to understand that, Sarah. I'm not the bad guy here."

She wanted to laugh, but she was too afraid. Anth was not an average bad guy bent on pain and suffering. He was quite literally insane. Just like Ace had been.

Isolation in a little shed? Had Ace tortured him

too? But he hadn't had Grandma Pauline or an older brother to save him. To tell him the truth about the good the world had to offer.

"Now, is this any way to talk to your brother for the first time, Sarah? I've been waiting to meet you. I've been looking forward to it."

Sarah didn't know what to say. She had her hand around the gun under the blanket, but she'd have to raise it and point it at him. He'd be able to fight her off before she did any of those things, especially if a contraction got in her way.

"I… I just found out about you."

"Ah. So your adopted family was full of liars." He laid the flashlight on the table next to her. It illuminated him and her heart twisted at how much he looked like a Wyatt. Dark hair, tall and broad-shouldered. But instead of the hazel eyes, he had blue eyes. Like hers. But there was no spark of life or warmth in those eyes. Only the fervor of someone who'd had a break with reality.

How was she supposed to handle that? Go along with what they had to say? "I suppose they were."

She was gratified when he nodded. He crouched down next to her, seemingly at ease with the situation. But there was a gun in his hand, and he pointed it at her head.

"I'm here to offer you an opportunity, Sarah. A chance. A test." He frowned at her stomach. "This does put a wrench in the plans, though."

"Maybe you could come back later."

He laughed. Threw his head back and laughed and

laughed. Sarah tightened her grip on the gun. He was too close now for her to maneuver the gun and get a shot off, but eventually *someone* would come to save her. She'd be able to shoot him if he turned around to fend off anyone who came in.

As long as a contraction didn't roll through her.

"Did you... Did you know your parents?" Sarah asked tremulously.

"Yes. I lived with our mother for a time. But she didn't understand me. She didn't *try* to understand me. She tried to mold me into so much less."

"C-could you tell me about our mother?" Sarah didn't have to fake the shake in her voice. The emotion. It was both fear and longing. And a desire to reach past his words into something real inside of him.

"She was stupid," he spat. "And selfish. She thought she was better than what Ace could give her. I showed her."

Sarah winced as another contraction began to steal over her. "You... What does that mean?"

"She thought she was sending me away to 'fix' me. An *institution*, Sarah. What mother sends their child to an institution? But Ace knew I was better than that. Ace knew. Sadly, even he outlived his use. He had to die for me to reach my full potential. They all did."

Sarah tried to blink away the tears, but they were falling too fast. "I don't. My baby doesn't have to die. I'll help you with whatever you need, Anth."

"That's exactly what she said. Our *mother*. Exactly the way she said it. You look just like her." Anth raised the gun, his face marred with a horrible sneer.

There was no humanity there. No hope of reaching something in his heart. If he'd ever had any compassion or sense of right or wrong, it had long since been twisted into this.

"I killed her," Anth said. "I had Ace killed. Killing you would be full circle, wouldn't it?" He glanced at her stomach again. "But there is the baby to consider. I know you're having a boy, Sarah. A boy who shares his blood with me. He could be mine."

"You need me alive to get him."

"I wouldn't count on it."

Sarah knew she had seconds at best. She wouldn't be able to get a shot off, but with the right leverage she could smack him in the face with the gun. She'd have to be quick—really quick before the contraction consumed her completely.

"Did you hear that?" she whispered, looking toward the kitchen.

He didn't lower the gun, didn't look toward the kitchen, but his eyebrows drew together. "No."

"Oh. Well then. Good." Sarah tried a fake smile. The contraction was tightening, tightening.

And slowly, oh so slowly, Anth inclined his head toward the kitchen ever so slightly. On a deep breath, Sarah used all her strength to lift the gun, blanket and all, and ram it into his face.

There was a sickening crunch, a scream of pain, but her own pain was overpowering. She lost her grip on the gun and it clattered to the floor.

DEV HAD CRAWLED his way across the snow toward the house. It was pitch black, so Anth must have cut the power. He made it to the back door, knowing he didn't have the strength to fight Anth—and didn't have a gun to shoot him with. He was shaking—both from being cold and wet and likely from blood loss.

But if he could get inside, there were guns. There was help. Surely the women inside could fight off one man. Had he really only been one man?

A man who was deluded enough to think he could take them down single-handedly. He couldn't. *Couldn't.*

Dev heard something, a scuffle or breath expelled. Something…odd. Off. He climbed for the stairs of the porch leading to the mudroom, leading to Sarah.

But he felt something in the snow. A body. "God." He reached out and felt what he could in the dark.

There was a low guttural swear.

"Brady?"

"Knocked us out," Brady rasped, then swore again. "Tied us together. Sarah's in labor. You don't have time to untie us. Go."

It felt all wrong to leave Brady tied up in the snow, but Sarah was in labor and there was no way to get them out of their bonds in the dark. He felt the body next to Brady and found what he'd hoped. Liza's cell phone.

"Is she going to be okay?" he asked Brady.

"I don't know, but I am, so that's a good sign."

Dev placed the phone in Brady's hands. "If you can get some kind of SOS message—"

"I'll see what I can do. Go!"

Dev didn't hesitate. He moved for the house. Every ounce of his body hurt. He was so cold he wasn't sure he'd survive this. But he couldn't die until he knew Sarah and the baby were safe.

In labor. Labor. Too much of a distraction. Too easy for Anth to infiltrate. Dev managed to make it to the mudroom door. Based on what he could feel in the dark it had been kicked open, splintered.

Dev felt his way through the mudroom, then the door to the kitchen, which had been given the same kicked-in treatment.

He could hear the sound of voices. Sarah's and… Anth's. If she kept him talking, and Dev had enough strength, he could maybe sneak into the living room and tackle Dev. He probably wouldn't win, but maybe he'd give everyone in the house a chance to help.

There was a scream of pain—a man's scream of pain. Followed by a woman's keening moan. Dev stumbled forward into the living room. There was a beam of light barely illuminating the far corner of the living room.

Anth was holding his face, screaming, and Sarah was writhing on the couch.

Anth turned toward Dev. Blood was gushing out of his nose—which was pointed in the wrong direction. His hand shook as he aimed the gun at Dev. But as long as he was aiming it at Dev again, he wasn't focusing on Sarah.

"I survived, Anth," Dev said. His vision was blurring and he wasn't sure his legs could hold him up much longer. But if he could talk, maybe Anth wouldn't shoot. "Isn't that a sign? Ace would have said I was meant for more to survive getting shot. To get back here."

"Ace was a fool," Anth said. He spit blood on the floor, then got to his feet. "You're a fool."

"You should have listened to Ace. You needed a lot more than just you to take us down. You can shoot me, Anth, but you won't make it out alive."

"You could have been better. You could have been—"

A gunshot exploded from behind Dev. Dev couldn't see who'd done it in the dark shadows, but Anth went down with a thud without another word.

Dev rushed forward. "Sarah."

She was crying and she grabbed on to him. "You're okay. You're okay. You're okay. The baby's coming. Is he dead?"

"I think so. We need to get you to the hospital."

"Ambulance coming. But it's snowy and…" Sarah wiped her nose with her sleeve then frowned at him. "Dev, you're bleeding."

"It's fine. I'm fine. I have to go get Brady and Liza. I have to… Who shot Anth?"

"I did." It was Grandma Pauline's voice. Frail and faraway-sounding. Dev jumped up and grabbed the flashlight. He pointed toward the voice. Grandma sat in the opposite corner of the room, small pistol in her hand, blood trickling down her head.

"Cecilia," she said, her voice weak.

It took Dev a minute to think through the shock to realize she was trying to yell at Cecilia.

Dev tried to get up, but his legs wouldn't hold him. Sarah was groaning in pain. "Cecilia. All clear," he called.

Immediately thundering footsteps sounded. Cecilia appeared and paled. "God. Nina! Nina, get down here! The girls will be okay. Get down here."

"Check if he's dead," Dev instructed. "Then go out to the porch. Brady is tied up but he's awake. I'm not sure about Liza. I…" His brain fumbled. It felt like the world was going gray.

"Dev? Dev?"

"It's okay. I'll be okay." He had to be okay. For Sarah. "The baby is coming."

"Yes. Yes. An ambulance is coming but the roads are bad and there were accidents and—"

"He's dead," Cecilia said flatly as Nina flew down the stairs, gun still at the ready.

"Grandma's hurt," Dev said, pointing to Grandma in the corner. Nina immediately rushed to her.

Cecilia stood and stalked away from Anth's body. "Are you sure he was alone?"

Dev nodded. "Yeah. Turns out one person can do a lot of damage with too much time alone to plan."

"I'll go get Brady. And the others. Then I'm going to call that ambulance again." She disappeared.

"Dev, come help me get Grandma up," Nina said. "We'll put her in the chair."

Dev tried to get to his feet. Tried to do anything to move away from where he was sitting next to Sarah on the couch. "I…can't."

"What? Why can't you?" Sarah demanded, hysteria tingeing her words.

Dev took her hand. He tried to tell her everything was going to be okay, but his throat was too tight. He pressed his forehead to her hand.

"Devin, you tell me right now what's going on."

He could hear the tears in her voice, hated that he'd put them there. "Anth managed to get a shot off. I'm okay. Just…a little hurt."

"Shot!" Sarah screeched.

But voices began to echo through the kitchen. Not just Cecilia and Brady. That was when Dev noticed flashing lights. The ambulance and fire department. God, thank *God*.

Weakness stole over him, but Sarah had a death grip on his hand. She was his anchor. Just like she'd always been. The thing that had kept him alive. Even when he'd been in that horrible darkness, it hadn't twisted into whatever had afflicted Anth.

Because he'd had her. And his brothers. His grandmother. Anth had been given a mother who had cared, who had tried. But it wasn't enough.

Dev would make sure it was enough for him. Always. So they all had to make it. *Had* to.

"She's in advanced labor," Brady said. He was leading a uniformed EMT over to Sarah with Cecilia's help.

"He's shot," Sarah said. "Dev's shot. Grandma's hurt. Please. Please, look at them. I'm okay." But the last word came out as if she was speaking through clenched teeth.

"We'll get to everyone," the EMT said calmly. "You don't worry about that."

The uniforms reminded Dev of what Anth had told him. "He'd befriended and paid off the deputy that was supposed to be our lookout. He's still out there."

"No, he's not," Jamison said. "I called the department for backup when I couldn't get a hold of him. He'd tried to speed away from here after the fire. He crashed. No word on his status, but it was a nasty wreck."

Dev blinked and looked around the room. An EMT was doing something to him he couldn't quite feel, which was probably bad. But his whole family was here. Bleeding. Dirty with smoke. Wet and frozen with cold.

But here. Alive. Breathing.

So he focused on being alive and breathing too. Pain sizzled through him as the paramedic dealt with his gunshot wound. The medic looked up at Dev. "Going to need to transport you, ASAP."

"Her first. Please."

The EMT looking over him glanced at the EMT checking out Sarah. She shook her head. "Afraid not. This baby is coming now."

Chapter Nineteen

Sarah wanted to scream. Dev was shot. Grandma Pauline was hurt. But they were focusing on *her*. No matter how she protested, there were people telling her to breathe, and then push.

The pain was unbearable.

"Don't let him die," she ground out, pushing with all her might.

"I'm not going to die," Dev said from somewhere behind her. They'd put him on a stretcher and were doing something to him back there, but she couldn't see.

She pushed and pushed and breathed when they told her to. She demanded Dev talk to her and she yelled at the EMTs to help Grandma Pauline, though apparently Brady was tending to her. But Brady had his own head wound, and so did Liza.

"What about the girls?" Sarah demanded after another excruciatingly painful push. If she focused on her fear for everyone else, she didn't think about the fact that she kept pushing and nothing was *happening*.

"You're doing great," the female EMT encouraged her. "One or two more and then the head will be out."

The head. Her baby's head. How was this happening? Cody had gotten the lights back on and the Christmas lights twinkled around her. Anth's body had been taken away. Those who hadn't been injured were taking turns taking showers and checking on the sleeping girls.

And she was having her baby. In Grandma Pauline's living room. After having survived a brush with a psychopath.

"Come on, Sarah. Push."

Nina was holding her hand, squeezing it. Someone was holding her legs, but she'd lost track of who and how. Which was probably for the best. She just pushed. Pushed and pushed and pushed.

"That's it. That's it. You're almost there. Deep breath, one more big one."

Sarah didn't know where she found the energy to push more. She would have sworn she was spent, and still she pushed. There was no choice. No way to stop this.

"That's it. That's it."

Pushed and pushed and felt the horrible, painful pressure slowly ease as she collapsed back into the couch.

"You did it. You did it. One more and he's out."

Sarah did everything they said. She heard her baby cry. The squirming mass of limbs was placed on the sterilized fabric they'd draped over her. She wasn't supposed to touch him yet, but she could feel his warmth, *him*.

"He's here," Sarah murmured, looking at her baby. Her son.

"And we need to load up and get to a hospital. We're going to wrap him up and take care of him, all right?"

Sarah nodded, because she couldn't speak. She could barely breathe. She was exhausted. Wrung out, and they'd taken her baby away. But he was here. Here and making noise. Alive. Safe.

"See him, daddy?" Sarah heard the EMT ask Dev. She managed to twist her head to see Dev get the first glimpse at their son.

Their son.

In the midst of terror and tragedy, a miracle had arrived.

PAUL KNIGHT WYATT was perfect. His smattering of hair was dark, his eyes were blue—which everyone told him would change, though Dev held out hope he had Sarah's eyes. Regardless, all eight pounds of him made up for everything that had been a part of his delivery.

Dev had not been able to hold his son, or kiss the love of his life, or anything important for the first few days. They'd been relegated to separate hospital rooms, where they could only communicate through video chats on their phones.

But they did those, regularly, even when the pain

meds made him a little loopy and one of his brothers had to hold the phone for him.

Sarah and Paul had gone home first. Paul, named after the woman who had saved Dev's life too many times to count. She'd shot Anth, and ended the nightmare. Just like she'd once welcomed him into her home, promising to keep him safe. And loved.

Grandma Pauline had beaten them all home, of course. Though she'd suffered a concussion, she'd been back at the ranch the next day. Liza had needed an extra day of observation because she'd had concussions before.

Everyone else who had battled the fire had been checked out for smoke inhalation, but had invariably been able to go home that night. Though Duke had stayed with Sarah since Dev couldn't.

It was eating him up inside.

When a nurse came in to check his vitals, he harassed her about going home. She patiently told him that was up to the doctors, but surgery following a gunshot wound was pretty serious.

He'd growled at her retreating back, scowling deeper when Jamison entered the room. "I am not in the mood for visitors."

"I wouldn't be so sure about that," Jamison said cheerfully. "I've arranged a little bit of a surprise for New Year's Eve, but it's not authorized, so you're going to have to be a good boy."

Dev only grunted.

"Trust me. You're going to want this surprise."

Brady came in, pushing a wheelchair in front of him. "Gage is distracting the nurses. Let's go."

Dev frowned at them. "You're not breaking me out."

"You're not ready to be broken out," Brady replied. Still, both his brothers helped him into the wheelchair, Brady manning the chair, Jamison pushing the IV cart. They put some blankets over his lap and draped a coat over his shoulders. "Now, don't say a word. Got it?"

Dev couldn't say he *did* get it, but his head and body ached, so he did what he was told as his brothers wheeled him through the hallway, to an elevator, then all the way down to the main floor. And right out the front doors.

"I thought you said you weren't breaking me out." It was cold, but sunny. Dev squinted against the bright sunlight after days of fluorescent lighting. Brady stood behind him, manning the wheelchair, but Jamison walked to the parking lot. To a truck.

His truck.

Sarah got out of the passenger seat and Jamison pulled a baby's car seat out of the back. Every grumpy, angry, pain-fueled thought emptied out of him as she came over, smiling.

"I thought you might like a chance to hold your baby."

Dev didn't trust his voice, so he just nodded. Jamison and Sarah fiddled with the car seat and wrapped the little bundle up in layers and layers.

After a few minutes, Sarah placed Paul in his arms.

She settled a blanket around both of them. "There's your daddy," she whispered to Paul. "We've been missing him. Haven't we?"

Paul was bundled head to toe, pretty much only his eyes and mouth showing. Those eyes were wide and alert and gazed right at Dev.

"Look at you," he murmured, bowled over, body and soul. Heart and mind. Just…blank because all he could do was stare at this baby—*his son*—and feel.

He had no idea how long he simply held his son against him and looked, tried to memorize every expression, every inch. Eventually he raised his gaze to the woman he loved. Who'd given birth to this baby on his grandmother's couch. Who'd survived and was standing there *smiling*. And he was just saturated with gratitude. With love. And hope. "Thank you," he managed to say, though his voice was rough.

"For giving birth?" she asked with a laugh. One hand rested on his shoulder, and the other gently touched Paul's cheek. "I didn't have much of a choice. He was coming out one way or another."

"No. Thank you for saving me."

She looked from Paul to him, smoothed the hair on his forehead. "You're muddled. Grandma Pauline did that."

"She saved my life, probably more than once all things said and done. But I'm not talking about that. I'm talking about…me. Without you, I'd still be… missing."

"Without us," Sarah said, nodding toward their son in his arms.

"Yeah. Yeah. We have to get married."

Her smile died, turning into a confused frown. "You couldn't even phrase it like a question?"

"Why would I do that?" He grinned up at her. "You're going to marry me." There were no doubts, and Dev wouldn't waste another second of his life.

Never again.

Epilogue

One Year Later

She married him. In a small intimate ceremony on the ranch as soon as Dev got out of the hospital. Their families, their dogs, their horses had been there as they'd promised to love and cherish each other forever.

They'd moved into the Knight house, since Grandma Pauline had Brady, Cecilia and later on baby Paula living with them.

Grandma Pauline had quite the array of great-grandchildren named after her.

They put to rest the ghosts of Ace and Anth—together and with their family. As another Christmas dawned, life was good.

Dev stepped into the mudroom and wiped his boots on the mat. He hung his coat up on the peg, shaking the snow off of it. His leg ached, but his wife had snuck out early and done most of the chores before he'd noticed she'd gone.

She'd let him handle the evening chores, and so

he'd gone out with his father-in-law and done the work of keeping the Reaves and Knight ranches running, even on Christmas.

When Duke had gone inside Grandma Pauline's, where the festivities would be, Dev had begged off a few minutes. The moon shone bright above. They'd had a blizzard last week so the entire area was covered in snow. Glittering, Christmasy snow.

He and Sarah had taken Paul out to play in it this morning, and Dev didn't know when he'd ever been so happy.

Actually, he did know. Never. Never in the whole of his life had he been able to access this well of happiness. Because he'd had brothers who'd sacrificed for him, a grandmother who'd given him a foundation to build on, but it had been Sarah and Paul who'd finally brought him to *this*.

The families had grown and the living room was packed. Nina and Cecilia had given birth to healthy girls. Jamison and Liza had adopted three siblings ranging in ages from five to fifteen. It wasn't smooth sailing, but Liza and Jamison were well-equipped to deal with the unique challenges of adopted older children touched by tragedy.

While Cash and Brownie lived with his family at the Knight ranch, Brady and Cecilia had adopted two dogs, and Rachel had gotten a guide dog. All five animals were curled in various spots around the house, because Grandma Pauline had shocked them all and lifted her ban on having animals in the house.

For the great-grandchildren's sake.

Dev took a moment to watch, to enjoy. Sarah had taught him how to do that too. When Paul caught sight of him, he let out a squeal and wriggled away from Sarah.

Dev grinned and crouched down, holding out his arms. "There's my guy. You going to walk to Daddy?"

Paul gurgled an answer, his hazel eyes lighting up with mischievousness. The boy got into everything, loved horses and dogs more than anything else, and held his parents' hearts in his small pudgy hands.

He was *this* close to taking his first steps.

Sarah picked him up and placed him on his feet. The boy bent his knees, over and over again, before taking one step forward. He immediately collapsed, but chortled merrily as his butt hit the ground. Then he crawled the rest of the way to Dev, squealing when Dev picked him up and gave him a little toss.

"Da!"

"You're going to be a walking machine before we know it, aren't you?"

Sarah came over to stand next to him. "I think we've got some major baby proofing to do then."

Paul babbled happily, flinging himself over to Sarah and then wiggling back down to the ground. He crawled over to Grandma Pauline and began babbling happily to her, one small hand resting on Cash's head.

Dev would have gladly slid his arm around Sarah's waist and enjoyed the moment, but Jamison came over.

"Come on," Jamison said, nodding toward the kitchen.

Dev frowned, but got to his feet and followed his

brothers back into the kitchen. Gage was getting beers out of the fridge, handing them out. Everyone except him and maybe Tucker seemed to know what was going on.

Though it dawned on Dev eventually that this is exactly what his brothers had done for him last year. Dev grinned.

"What are we doing?" Tucker asked.

"We're inducting our newest member," Jamison said with mock seriousness. "Welcome, Tuck. You've officially joined our ranks."

All eyes turned to Tucker.

"What are you guys… Wait. You know?" He frowned. "Who told?"

"Your wife isn't great at keeping secrets," Gage offered. "And neither am I, since I was the one who overheard her telling Felicity."

"And spread the word," Tucker said disgustedly.

"Just to the club," Jamison said, raising his beer bottle. "The father's club. Welcome."

Tucker rubbed his fist over his chest. "Is it going to be this terrifying the whole time?"

"Worse," Dev offered.

"And worse and worse and worse," Cody added. "I'm going to have to survive two girls going through puberty, Tucker. Nothing is as terrifying as that."

They laughed and chatted, razzed Tucker about the coming responsibilities and sleepless nights. It was good, and it was right, but Dev couldn't help but think about last year. There had been so much terror and pain and suffering. He wanted to commemorate that somehow. How far they'd come from six scared boys in their father's gang.

"You know, it's been a year now," Dev said. "A year of peace and stability, aside from the fear of puberty and whatnot. We've…had to fight a lot to get here."

"Survived a lot to get here," Gage said.

"Yes, we have," Jamison agreed. He smiled, raising his bottle. "And now we get to live."

Dev clinked his bottle with his brothers. As toasts went, it was the best he could think of. He glanced into the other room, where their wives and grandmother, the women who'd helped save them in a variety of different ways, sat with their children.

So that they could be here.

Living.

Which was finally exactly where Dev Wyatt wanted to be.

* * * * *

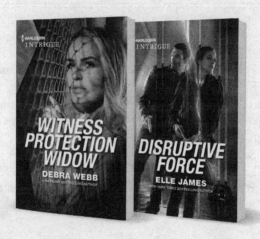

Makena needed medical attention. That part was obvious. The tricky part was going to be getting her looked at. He was still trying to wrap his mind around the fact Makena Eden was sitting in his SUV.

Talk about a blast from the past and a missed opportunity. But he couldn't think about that right now when she was injured. At least she was eating. That had to be a good sign.

When she'd tried to stand, she'd gone down pretty fast and hard. She'd winced in pain and he'd scooped her up and brought her to his vehicle. He knew better than to move an injured person. In this case, however, there was no choice.

The victim was alert and cognizant of what was going on. A quick visual scan of her body revealed nothing obviously broken. No bones were sticking out. She complained about her hip and he figured there could be something there. At the very least, she needed an X-ray.

Since getting to the county hospital looked impossible at least in the short run and his apartment was close by, he decided taking her to his place might be for the best until the roads cleared. He could get her out of his uncomfortable vehicle and onto a soft couch.

Normally, he wouldn't take a stranger to his home, but this was Makena. And even though he hadn't seen her in forever, she'd been special to him at one time.

He still needed to check on the RV for Mrs. Dillon...and then it dawned on him. Was Makena the "tenant" the widow had been talking about earlier?

"Are you staying in town?" he asked, hoping to get her to volunteer the information. It was possible that she'd fallen on hard times and needed a place to hang her head for a couple of nights.

"I've been staying in a friend's RV," she said. So, she was the "tenant" Mrs. Dillon had mentioned.

It was good seeing Makena again. At five feet five inches, she had a body made for sinning underneath a thick head of black hair. He remembered how shiny and wavy her hair used to be. Even soaked with water, it didn't look much different now.

She had the most honest set of pale blue eyes—eyes the color of the sky on an early summer morning. She had the kind of eyes that he could stare into all day. It had been like that before, too.

But that was a long time ago. And despite the lightning bolt that had struck him square in the chest when she turned to face him, this relationship was purely professional.

Don't miss
Texas Law *by Barb Han,*
available December 2020 wherever
Harlequin Intrigue books and ebooks are sold.

Harlequin.com

HIEXP1120

Get 4 FREE REWARDS!

We'll send you 2 FREE Books
<u>plus</u> 2 FREE Mystery Gifts.

Harlequin Intrigue books are action-packed stories that will keep you on the edge of your seat. Solve the crime and deliver justice at all costs.

FREE
Value Over
$20

YES! Please send me 2 FREE Harlequin Intrigue novels and my 2 FREE gifts (gifts are worth about $10 retail). After receiving them, if I don't wish to receive any more books, I can return the shipping statement marked "cancel." If I don't cancel, I will receive 6 brand-new novels every month and be billed just $4.99 each for the regular-print edition or $5.99 each for the larger-print edition in the U.S., or $5.74 each for the regular-print edition or $6.49 each for the larger-print edition in Canada. That's a savings of at least 12% off the cover price! It's quite a bargain! Shipping and handling is just 50¢ per book in the U.S. and $1.25 per book in Canada.* I understand that accepting the 2 free books and gifts places me under no obligation to buy anything. I can always return a shipment and cancel at any time. The free books and gifts are mine to keep no matter what I decide.

Choose one: ☐ **Harlequin Intrigue**   ☐ **Harlequin Intrigue**
                  Regular-Print   **Larger-Print**
                  (182/382 HDN GNXC)   (199/399 HDN GNXC)

Name (please print)

Address   Apt. #

City   State/Province   Zip/Postal Code

Email: Please check this box ☐ if you would like to receive newsletters and promotional emails from Harlequin Enterprises ULC and its affiliates. You can unsubscribe anytime.

Mail to the **Reader Service:**
IN U.S.A.: P.O. Box 1341, Buffalo, NY 14240-8531
IN CANADA: P.O. Box 603, Fort Erie, Ontario L2A 5X3

Want to try 2 free books from another series? Call 1-800-873-8635 or visit www.ReaderService.com.

---

*Terms and prices subject to change without notice. Prices do not include sales taxes, which will be charged (if applicable) based on your state or country of residence. Canadian residents will be charged applicable taxes. Offer not valid in Quebec. This offer is limited to one order per household. Books received may not be as shown. Not valid for current subscribers to Harlequin Intrigue books. All orders subject to approval. Credit or debit balances in a customer's account(s) may be offset by any other outstanding balance owed by or to the customer. Please allow 4 to 6 weeks for delivery. Offer available while quantities last.

Your Privacy—Your information is being collected by Harlequin Enterprises ULC, operating as Reader Service. For a complete summary of the information we collect, how we use this information and to whom it is disclosed, please visit our privacy notice located at corporate.harlequin.com/privacy-notice. From time to time we may also exchange your personal information with reputable third parties. If you wish to opt out of this sharing of your personal information, please visit readerservice.com/consumerschoice or call 1-800-873-8635. **Notice to California Residents**—Under California law, you have specific rights to control and access your data. For more information on these rights and how to exercise them, visit corporate.harlequin.com/california-privacy.

HI20R2